I tr...   n's
doppelg...   ılar
traffic th...   on
Grafton. I fall in step behind her and panic for a split second when I momentarily lose sight of her, but then the hair darts left onto Duke Street and into a place called Davy Byrnes.

I loiter outside the pub with the oddly familiar name.

Well, here goes nothing.

I casually stroll through the mostly empty pub like a detective looking for a missing person. My gaze scours the entire establishment, but I don't spot the mystery woman.

She's got to be in here, so I will wait it out.

After sitting on a stool where I can see almost every high-traffic area, the bartender asks with a fabulous Irish accent, "What'll it be, love?"

"What kind of soft drinks do you have?" I absently inquire while combing through my wallet for money.

"For minerals, I have cola, lemon lime, orange, and of course, beer and whiskey if you feel so inclined."

"Orange, please."

"As you wish." He fills a glass with ice and places it in front of me along with an open glass bottle. I hand him three euros, and when his hazel eyes meet mine, he slaps his palm against his forehead. "Go way outta that, weren't you over by Parnell Square earlier today?"

I am face to face with the chestnut-haired puddle jumper I encountered in front of the Dublin Writers Museum.

To Kelly—

Enduring the Waves

by

Jill Ocone

Learn from life's waves & enjoy the ride!

Jill Ocone

This is a work of fiction. Names, characters, places, and incidents are either the product of the author's imagination or are used fictitiously, and any resemblance to actual persons living or dead, business establishments, events, or locales, is entirely coincidental.

Enduring the Waves

COPYRIGHT © 2023 by Jill Ocone

All rights reserved. No part of this book may be used or reproduced in any manner whatsoever without written permission of the author or The Wild Rose Press, Inc. except in the case of brief quotations embodied in critical articles or reviews.
Contact Information: info@thewildrosepress.com

Cover Art by *Tina Lynn Stout*

The Wild Rose Press, Inc.
PO Box 708
Adams Basin, NY 14410-0708
Visit us at www.thewildrosepress.com

Publishing History
First Edition, 2023
Trade Paperback ISBN 978-1-5092-5219-0
Digital ISBN 978-1-5092-5220-6

Published in the United States of America

Dedication

For Tara Gardner and Nicholas Ott. Thank you.

Acknowledgments

Thank you to Wild Rose Press for taking a chance on a debut novelist, and to my editor, Judi Mobley, for her exceptional insight and assistance.

To my husband, Tony, thank you for your love and support. I love you with all my heart.

To my family (Emily, Nicholas, Harrison, Isaac, Aniina, Ross, Nicole, Hannah, AJ, Mom, Mom, Dusty, and Maria), thank you for believing in me. I love you all.

To my lifelong best friends, Jennifer Gerics, Laura Kerwin, and Noreen O'Donnell, thank you for always being there.

To George Valente, none of these words would exist without you. Thank you.

To my Hawk family (especially Tracey Raimondo, Mandi Bean, Danielle Palmieri, Heather Staples, Michelle Masi, Erin Berhalter, Gerry O'Donnell, Christine Wolfman, Tracy Ritchey, Patty Goley, Will Schmidt, Linda Saraceno, Lisa Vecchione, Michael Statile, Kaitlyn Kettmann, and Val Kohan), to my Rise and Write writing group, and to Marjon Weber, Carol Moroz, Marci Strauss, and the DeFelice 5, thank you for your role along my journey.

To you, the reader, thank you for choosing to read *Enduring the Waves*. I hope you find a kernel of inspiration within its pages and connect with Kelly's story.

Part One: The Past, or Life

"Hold to the now, the here, through which all future plunges to the past."
James Joyce, *Ulysses*
Chapter One
I couldn't help but skip as I strolled out of the brick-faced school building into the gloriously extraordinary early-September day during what we refer to as "local summer" here at the Jersey Shore.

Mother Nature's deliciousness, what a dish for the senses she served up with her recipe for the five-star afternoon. The balmy breeze delicately painted the wispy white clouds like feathers in the dreamy sapphire bowl above me while the sweet, late-summer goldenrods' fragrance sailing along the air's currents seduced my nostrils. For a moment, I longed to curl my toes in the sand at the water's edge near Smuggler's Inlet with the other locals soaking up one of the last moments of pure bliss before the autumn's winds arrived. That fancy passed quickly, though, as I delighted in this alternative setting, which was one I had worked damn hard to enjoy.

A football player wearing a black jersey with the school's Stingray mascot embellished on the sleeves in metallic silver jogged past me on his way to practice, his plastic cleats crunching on the pavement with each of his forward strides. "See you in tomorrow's class, Ms. Lynch," he yelled while waving his dinged helmet in the air.

I recognized his face from sitting somewhere in the middle of my classroom earlier, but I couldn't recall his name from the list of almost one hundred students on my rosters. I shouted back a generic "Have a great practice" through an involuntary smile pulling my cheekbones tight.

If anyone told me five years ago I'd be a high school English teacher today, I never would have believed him and insisted there was no way in hell it would ever happen.

Fat chance.

Zero possibility.

But I would have been as wrong as a Y2K conspiracy theorist.

Having religiously booed the Stingrays as an Oldentown Beach High School Otter back when my CD player rotated between my favorite boy band songs, I adopted a new loyalty as Waterville High School's newest faculty member. The legendary rivalry between the two high schools formed in the early 1950s when the growing teenage population of Seacove County split between the "old" school, my alma mater of Oldentown Beach, and the "new" school, Waterville.

My life was one futile escape attempt after another, but once I finally got my shit together, I took college classes for three years at night while clocking in forty hours a week at InformationTech as a data entry specialist. I graduated with my bachelor's degree in English education in May on a day much like today, beautiful and warm and full of promise, albeit a few years later than expected. Each stroke of my fingertips over the embossed, glossy green letters spelling out K-e-l-l-y L-y-n-c-h in Old English script on my college diploma erased part of the word "failure" I formerly wore around my neck like an albatross to the point where just a faint stencil remained.

I spent my spring and summer responding to every high school English teacher vacancy advertisement I could find with a cover letter and my resume. After two interviews and a mock lesson about the themes of ambition and guilt in William Shakespeare's "Macbeth," the principal of Waterville High School selected me from at least fifty other candidates to fill the one full-time position available, and the board of education gave me their seal of approval at their August meeting.

My new department colleagues welcomed me into their tribe on staff orientation day with a beautiful basket brimming with all kinds of school supplies teachers go crazy for: markers and sticky notes and "Way To Go" stickers and the like, as well as a plate engraved with my name and classroom number in the school's iconic silver and black to hang next to my door in the hallway.

A stroke of scheduling luck gave me and Shannon Moran, my favorite and the spunkiest of the bunch, the same planning and lunch periods and all the junior British Literature classes. She told me I would remember my first day of school as a teacher for the rest of my life.

I had a hunch she was correct.

I tossed my new teal school satchel onto the back seat of my car and surveyed the landscape with the warm sun beaming down on me: the impeccably manicured lush green athletic fields, the lone yellow bus with the sputtering engine idling in the lot, the butterfly garden's lavender and orange blooms bordering the outdoor cafeteria pavilion, every stately silver letter that spelled out "Waterville High School" above the main entrance shimmering from the sun's reflection. The boys' cross-country team dashed down Davis Drive just as cheers and whistles from the girls' soccer scrimmage frolicked in my ears, not unlike the melodies trickling into the hall from the music room while on my duty rounds earlier today.

I exhaled deeply through my childlike grin.

I was home.

Not the same way I felt when I arrived home at our townhouse. I opened the door to find Wayne holding a sweating amber bottle at the ready for me. "Well, Mrs. Coopersmith, or should I say Ms. Lynch, you certainly are beaming," he half complimented, half jeered with a crooked, cynical smirk and the stale smell of swill already on his breath.

I handed off my satchel to him instead of accepting the beer. "The best day of my life."

"How can today top the day you met me"—he cocked his head—"or the day we got married?"

I kicked off my shoes as the rock forming in the pit of my stomach expanded. "No, today was a different kind of special. In my first period class, let's see, there was Laurie, and Kaitlyn, and Trevor…oh, he was the football player who ran past me. And Shannon helped me write my lesson objectives for when we begin 'Beowulf' tomorrow."

" 'Beowulf'?" Wayne rolled his eyes. "Who needs that crap?" The beads of condensation almost caused the bottle to slip out of his hand, but he steadied it just in time and held it out to me. "Here, you earned it."

I avoided eye contact with him and gathered what I needed from my bag. "I have a lot to do to prepare for tomorrow. Please, Wayne, I'd much rather celebrate my first day of teaching by going out to grab a quick bite with you."

"You know, you were a lot more fun when you were the party girl," he grumbled. "Even though you don't have to work, I'll drink your beer to celebrate. And what's wrong with getting delivery?" He downed in one gulp the bottle of beer I twice refused.

"Take out is fine. Give me a yell when you are ready to order."

My heart sank as we headed in opposite directions as usual, him to the kitchen for another bottle and me to the Smuggler's room. I closed the door behind me, and with my back against it, I took a few deep breaths to center myself.

My favorite place in the world was Smuggler's Inlet. If I had a nickel for every word I wrote there before they stopped flowing, I'd probably be a millionaire. Smuggler's was my refuge, and like my notebooks used to be, my therapist.

I fell under Wayne's spell the moment my eyes connected with his alluring sea glass blues six years ago, and they hypnotized me more with every beer I drank. We experienced a day full of "firsts" soon after meeting: the first time he promised me a whole new world, the night we first slept together, and the first time the room he referred to as his "Smuggler's Escape" lured me into its depths.

The floor resembled a boardwalk with washed wood planks from wall to wall yet left nary a foot splinter, unlike the real boardwalks' rough boards. The furniture's oceanic hues balanced the room's seaside ambiance to perfection: an aquamarine blue sofa with velvety cushions, an indigo desk chair, turquoise and seafoam green bed linens and curtains, a plush rug with the appearance of real waves weaved into its lamblike fibers, bookcases and shelves crafted by hand from reclaimed wood, and an antique desk that could have served as a pirate captain's command post.

The sea's divine scent dappled the air, courtesy of a concealed fragrance diffuser, but the room's most impressive aspect was the painted mural of Smuggler's Inlet encircling it.

If life could be as perfect as depicted within those four walls.

Hundreds of lights twinkled in the sunrise on the ceiling to give the appearance of dawn's lingering stars. The artist captured everything one might actually see at the real Smuggler's: the anglers along the inlet's wall with their fishing rods bobbing in the current, the red and green signal lights atop the beacons at each jetty's end glowing with tiny light bulbs, a scallop boat with its outriggers dragging its nets where the sea meets the sky, the surfboard noses extending from behind the rocks across the way in Glenharbor, the portal to the sea with two surfers riding its breakers, a variety of seabirds flying in the air or standing on top of the welcome sign or stealing a snapper fish from the little boy's red bucket, the ponytailed writer silhouetted by the moon sitting on the flat rock jutting out the furthest…

Wayne told me on our first date when we parked at Smuggler's about one summer night when the full moon rose from the horizon behind a girl with a ponytail. She sat on the rock nearest the water, and the moon surrounded her as she wrote in a notebook. She transformed into a momentary black figure encircled by light, then she disappeared as the moon climbed higher in the sky. "She was an angel and even shows up in my dreams sometimes," he said. His mother commissioned the artist to paint the mural for Wayne's birthday with strict instructions to include the Smuggler's angel from his dreams.

It was me, no doubt about it.

That rock was my go-to writing spot, and the timeline matched up with the summer after I graduated high school. I spent every waking minute at Smuggler's that summer fantasizing about how much my life would improve at college and penning those thoughts in my notebook, which would meet its final fireplace fate a few weeks later.

But me?

An angel?

The girl of someone's dreams?

Please.

And what were the odds I'd actually meet the poor, misguided sap who thought of me as such, so much so my likeness became a permanent part of a room which was now my second-favorite place in the world, and modeled after my first-favorite place in the world?

I changed into my new Waterville t-shirt and light gray sweat shorts, then gawked at my silhouetted writing replica hidden within the mural like Waldo as I pulled my hair into a ponytail like hers.

She had such dreams, that girl with the notebook, so many possibilities and opportunities lying ahead of her, and she threw them all away.

Despite the day's numerous victories, I wallowed in defeat.

Wayne, he thrived on idleness and alcohol, and was

complacent with his mother footing our bills and living expenses from the massive inheritance she received from his father's fatal workplace accident shortly after Wayne's second birthday. Neither of them could understand why I wanted more out of life than lazy days and drunken nights, hence his jab about not having to work. The fact he still wanted me to change back into my old, soused self, well...

My students, as his sea glass blues and my words used to be, my students were now my light.

They had to be, or the last three years were all for nothing.

Shannon's advice to journal about my day in the classroom flitted through my thoughts, so I waded through the muck left behind by my decades-long writing drought and wrote two mediocre paragraphs from memory and the snippets of my day I jotted on sticky notes.

I flung my notebook aside and scanned my students' information surveys, noting birthdays, goals, and the academic strengths and weaknesses they chose to share with me. When I shifted my attention to fine tuning tomorrow's "Beowulf" lesson, a raucous yet muffled grunt from behind the door interrupted my train of thought.

"I'll be right out," I snapped.

I glanced at the clock and saw it was almost nine. I hadn't eaten anything nourishing since breakfast, so I headed to the living room. Wayne was already out cold on the sofa with a delivery menu from Antonio's underneath his hand.

I shook my head and shrugged my shoulders.

Maybe today wasn't as life changing as I thought,

after all.

****

I navigated my silver sedan into the empty faculty parking lot well before sunrise with a handful of stars dimly shimmering in the blue-hour sky. I strode into the building with a bounce in my step and flicked on my classroom lights. For a brief moment, I squinted from their brightness, then I breathed in deep the pleasing aroma of semi-old books combined with the twinge of typical musty classroom and a dose of after-the-rain scent emanating from the three gelatinous green cones I spaced around the room.

After I emptied my school satchel and stored my lunch bag under my desk, I watered the two young ivy plants on the windowsill. "You'll be crawling up along the glass panes in no time"—I whispered to them while giggling—"and soon you'll each be as long as the hallway."

I made my way back to my desk and pressed my computer's power button. As I waited for the monitor to liven with light, I pinched myself to make sure this was real.

Was I finally on the right track?

I stayed well after dismissal time on both pre-first-day-of-school in-service days to create an aesthetically pleasing yet functional classroom by infusing my love of the ocean with paper resembling the sea covering my bulletin boards and trimming them with scalloped borders full of colorful sea stars. I even found a small rubber-backed floor mat and a roll of ribbon both with a similar sea star design in the clearance section of the local discount department store. I placed the mat underneath the pencil sharpener screwed to the wall and adorned the "take a pen or pencil" containers I crafted from clear mason jars with the ribbon. I also used the ribbon as a hanger for the seashell "Welcome" wreath on my classroom door after I removed its generic wire loop which resembled a mangled fishing hook.

"Hey, you." Shannon strolled in and lobbed a shiny red apple to me just as I finished copying my agenda onto the whiteboard with a black dry erase marker. "You deserve this apple for being so chipper at this ungodly hour. How was your first day?"

"Yesterday was amazing"—I flashed her a broad smile—"and I have a hunch today will be even better. Thanks for the apple."

"There's more where that came from. You're so lucky you'll never know what it's like to get chalk all over your clothes first thing in the morning. These whiteboards are such a godsend. Do you need anything or have any questions before I prep for the day?"

I hesitated for a minute, then I hit my forehead with my palm. "Yes, I do have a question. You showed me another copy machine besides the one in the library, but I can't remember where. I'm set for today as far as worksheets go, but someone hung an 'out of order' sign on the library copier yesterday and I need to make copies for tomorrow."

"Already? That piece of shit is always down," Shannon scoffed. "The other copier is in the mailroom between the main office and the counseling suite. I'll swing by to pick you up for lunch, okay? You can't skip lunch like you did yesterday. We're all busy, but we all need to eat, too."

"Sounds great. Thanks for keeping an eye on me."

"No problem, Kel. I'll see you later." The post-sunrise's rays streaming through the classroom skylights ignited her shamrock-green eyes and her necklace's three wave-like swirls as she spun around, her ginger locks fanning out then settling at her shoulders as she headed across the hall to her classroom.

I gasped, and my apple hit the floor with a thud then rolled under my desk.

Those swirls...

During the summer between high school and college, I was up at Smuggler's writing, which wasn't unusual, but I'll never forget one particular evening. The sun descending in the west transformed the sky into a tapestry of colors with every imaginable hue stretching over its ribbonlike clouds and unlike any end-of-day splendor I had ever seen. As night absorbed the last sliver of purple, I swore the waves below me whispered, "The light, it shines ahead, Kelly. Someday, you'll find it."

With the sea's breeze caressing my cheeks and goosebumps spilling over my skin, my eye caught something glimmering on the ground which was illuminated by a car's headlights behind me. I took the little pewter pendant with three engraved spiral-like swirls that resembled ocean waves into my hand and foolishly carried the bauble as a keepsake of the message from the water, to never abandon my pursuit of the light.

I dug the pendant out of my dress pocket and my mouth dropped. The same symbol dangled from Shannon's necklace.

The three swirls had to mean something, but what?

My mind's wheel revolved with the possibility I might be onto something, but the echoes of bustling students and lockers being jarred open and slammed shut returned me to the present. I scribbled "apple from

Shannon, the swirls" on a sticky note, then picked up my bruised offering from Shannon off the floor and placed the assignments I needed to copy in my satchel.

I straightened the one out-of-place desk to make the rows perfect on my way to take my perch at my classroom door. I quizzed myself on my seating charts and names to divert my attention from my pounding heart. When the first student in my first period class arrived, I greeted her with, "Emily Isaacson, right?"

Emily's eyes brightened and she hooted, "Wow, you remember my name and it's only the second day of school." She gave me a high five, then when she got to her desk, she breathed in in deep and said, "It smells super good in here."

One down, twenty-three to go.

My classroom rapidly filled, and I passed my test by going twenty-four for twenty-four in successfully remembering everyone's name. After reciting the Pledge of Allegiance, my students engaged in a writing task about ethics to prepare for their "Beowulf" lesson.

I taught three classes in what felt like ten minutes, then Shannon retrieved me for lunch as she promised.

"Why is it so empty in here?" I asked as I slid a chair with a torn goldenrod cushion out from under the table, its metal legs harshly scraping against the faculty lunch room's blemished floor tiles.

Shannon answered as she unpacked her lunch bag. "It's a by-product of having first lunch, there's usually only a handful of us. I was assigned first lunch last year, too, just me and Al Myers, the weasel."

"I don't think I've met him yet."

"Probably not, because you'd know who I mean if you did. Al is a smarmy math teacher and complains more than the teenage girls we teach. I ended up eating by myself in my classroom because he sucked the life right out of me, and the silver lining was I didn't have to subject myself to this late-1970s ski lodge lobby decor."

She paused spreading butter on her blueberry muffin and gestured toward the peeling brown, orange, and olive-green rainbow on the innermost wall. "I think the art teacher plans to have her seniors repaint that atrocity as part of their portfolio project this year, and it's about time." She tore off a bit of her muffin and handed it to me. "Here, try this. It's the best butter out there."

I took one bite and would have sunk into my seat if it wasn't made from petrified pleather. "You're right, this is damn good butter."

"It's Kerrygold, the only brand I buy. Imported straight from the Emerald Isle."

I made a mental note to add Kerrygold butter to my shopping list.

Shannon took a sip of water then posed, "Forgive me for snooping, but when I glanced at the information form you filled out with your husband listed as your emergency contact, I noticed the difference in your last names and was curious about why you don't use his."

I rarely shared the sundry details of my checkered past, but I had a strong inkling Shannon wouldn't judge me. "Truth is, I shacked up with Wayne after knowing him for like a few hours, and a few weeks later, we ended up at the Waterville Court House one afternoon after killing a thirty pack and a fifth of whiskey. In my drunken stupor, I signed my maiden name on the marriage certificate where I was supposed to sign my married name. The paperwork hassle to legally change my name afterward was a nightmare, so I never did it."

"The court actually married you, as drunk as you were?"

"Wayne's mother, Moira, she knows just about everyone in town, so the Justice of the Peace's secretary contacted her to make sure we were on the up and up. She demanded he wait, and she soon came running in with a photographer and a giant bottle of champagne. She insisted he marry us right then and there or she'd have him fired, so he married us. My so-called dream wedding." I sighed. "I guess it's a good thing I barely remember it."

Shannon nodded to show she was listening, so I continued, "We would drink from sunup to sundown every day, Wayne and I, even more than I did during my last semester at Gardner College. One night, we were at Antonio's for dinner with Moira. I didn't drink because I was recovering from the flu, but both were blotto before we finished our salads. It was the first time I was on the side of witnessing, instead of partaking in, the slurring and yelling and the haphazard flinging of linguine and clam sauce all over the place, then Moira knocked over the dessert cart while staggering back from the restroom."

"How classy. Glad I wasn't eating there that night."

"The incident was incredibly embarrassing"—I shook my head—"and I wanted to disappear. The other customers were disgusted, and so was I, but the manager's hands were tied because Moira was one of the main donors to the owner's non-profit foundation. The toppled dessert cart sparked an awakening in me. Wayne, he still drinks." Heat spilled over my cheeks as our eyes connected. "Geez, I'm sorry if I laid too much on you, everything just came out."

"You can confide in me anytime, Kel. I give you credit for taking control of your life."

"It's no big deal, I just did what I had to do." I waved my hand in front of me then asked, "The pendant on your necklace caught my eye this morning. Does it mean anything?"

"Which one am I wearing?" she wondered as she fondled the three silver swirls. "Oh, the triskele. My sister, Deirdre, gave this to me when I graduated from Notre Dame. It's an ancient Celtic symbol."

I passed her my tarnished Smuggler's charm. "I found this years ago at Smuggler's Inlet, and I never encountered another one like it until today. The swirls always looked like three ocean waves to me."

"Yup, yours is a bit beat up, but it's a triskele, all right. Come to think of it, the spirals do resemble sea waves. I never realized that before. Deirdre is a big believer in symbols and legends. When she gave the necklace to me, she said it was time for me to move forward, which is what the three spirals meant to her, the energy to face life head on and make it happen, kind of like you did by becoming a teacher."

I nodded. "Makes sense. Now that I enlightened you about my refined and elegant wedding, tell me. Do you have a partner? Boyfriend? Girlfriend?"

Shannon stuck out her empty ring finger and impishly exclaimed, "Yes, and for crying out loud, I can't wait for the ring bling. My Oliver and I have been together for a little over two years now. We moved in together over the summer and he works in the city." She wrinkled her face and her tone of voice lowered. "My high school sweetheart, we dated for seven years. He teaches here, too, but when I met Oliver, I broke it off with him."

"Working in the same building as your ex has to be awkward, I'm sure."

"It's even more awkward when he's being an assclown, which lately, has been all the time."

I swirled my spoon in my nearly empty yogurt container and casually posed, "So, this former beau you speak of, have I met him yet?"

The bell blared before she could answer, and we both vaulted from our seats as I squealed, "We're going to be late." We grabbed our belongings and sprinted toward our respective classrooms in a fit of laughter.

****

"Everyone, add Neena's example of Beowulf's ethics to your chart. Our hero chooses to travel and help Hrothgar's people because he knows he can defeat the monster, Grendel. Deciding to go to Denmark with the blessings of his people is the right thing for Beowulf to do." I circled the room and handed a sticky note to every student. "Now, write your name and something you'll take away from today's lesson on your exit sticky and slap it on the door trim as you leave."

The classroom buzzed with activity and a few students were still writing when the last bell of the school day rang. Feet shuffled from desks to the hallway and hands smacked the metal trim for about twenty seconds, then I plucked the notes off one at a time after the room silenced.

Warmth flooded my heart as I read each, my students' participation in their first day of lessons reassuring me I was in the right place.

Shannon bounded into my room as I finished checking off the notes in my gradebook. "Hey, you, those stickies are a great way to wrap up a lesson." She slid a binder across my desk. "After we finish 'Beowulf,' we need to divide and conquer what we cover because there aren't enough books for both of us to teach the same piece of literature at the same time. The binder is full of resources for the short story unit. My classes will read 'Macbeth,' and if you take the short stories, we can swap when we finish."

"What short stories are in the curriculum again?" I questioned as I paged through the binder.

"There's 'No Witchcraft for Sale' by Doris Lessing, 'My Oedipus Complex' by Frank O'Connor, and 'Araby' by James Joyce the genius."

I crinkled up my nose. "Joyce? Really?"

Shannon stared at me like I had a horn growing out of the middle of my forehead. "I thought every English teacher loved Joyce. You've read him, right?"

"My junior English teacher assigned *A Portrait of the Artist as a Young Man*. My mother, she wouldn't hear of it, because she thought Joyce was a pervert, but it might have been just another ploy to exercise control over me. I had to independently read *Ethan Frome* instead and submit a reading journal every day. Man, I hated *Ethan Frome*." I pretended to gag by putting my finger near my mouth and continued. "One of my professors at Sullivan assigned *Portrait*, but I skimmed just enough to complete my paper because I was pressed for time. A classmate suggested I eventually read *Ulysses* since I planned to teach high school English, but I haven't gotten around to it just yet." Her green eyes bulged, so I added, "I sense I may have stepped on hallowed ground, here. My apologies."

Shannon rationalized her horrified countenance in

the manner of a litigator and loudly countered, "So, James Joyce is the one on trial here. You say you hate him, but you haven't given him a chance. He said, 'The demand that I make of my reader is that he should devote his whole life to reading my works,' and I, Shannon Moran, have done just that. As his defense attorney, it will be my job to convince you, Kelly Lynch, that the legendary Dubliner is the supreme literati, and I predict one day you will concur the all-knowing, pompous bloke changed your life." She thrust her right arm into the air with her index finger extended. "I titled my college English thesis 'Joyce: The Every-Man in Every One,' so I've got the evidence, my friend. I've got the proof. And you will acknowledge the astonishing brilliance that is James Joyce and experience firsthand his extraordinary influence." Shannon then slammed her pen onto a desk like a gavel and yelled, "All rise!"

I jumped to my feet and applauded. "Well done, counselor. Your testimony has swayed me to keep an open mind as I undergo your James Joyce tutelage. I should probably begin with him, then?"

"Definitely. Most students end up preferring 'Araby' over the other two stories, anyway, and it's best to kick off a new unit with something they'll like. There's theme and literary device resources, comprehension questions, and writing prompts in the binder. Modify for your students as you see fit. In the meantime, let's figure out our writing and 'Beowulf' tasks for the rest of the unit."

We sat down to work, and I followed Shannon's lead in drafting objectives and incorporating standards into my lessons and assignments. After we finished revising the "Beowulf" essay instructions, Shannon complimented, "You weren't kidding, Kel. You really are insightful with crafting writing prompts and thinking of fresh ways to assess student learning."

I fiddled with my pen. "I used to love to write and wanted to be a writer when I was a kid, but…"

"But what?"

"Long story for another time. I started my journal to document my first year of teaching as you suggested, even though it was a little difficult to get the words flowing again."

"One of my biggest regrets, but you learning from my mistake makes up for it. I'm impressed by your prompts. Maybe there's a little Joyce in you after all."

I playfully whined, "Him again?"

"Of course. It always circles back to Joyce." Shannon gave me a knowing glance and gathered her belongings. "The to-do list of an English teacher can sometimes be overwhelming, but don't abandon your urge to write. Release those words and cleanse your soul. And don't forget about Fridays, either. Everyone goes to Delancy's after school, even the coaches swing by after their practices or games. It's fun, and not everybody drinks, either. You should come."

"Maybe I will. Thanks again, Shan."

"My pleasure. Catch you tomorrow." As she bounced out of the room, I couldn't help but be a tad bit jealous of her confidence and end-of-day vigor.

Friday at Delancy's. It would be nice to do something with others, for once, and a good way to get acquainted with my coworkers outside the classroom.

Yes.

I decided to go to Delancy's.

****

The unfamiliar rhythm of my school day schedule soon harmonized into a satisfying routine. I stayed until about half past four on Mondays through Thursdays to grade and prepare for the following day's lessons right in my classroom because I focused better with the necessary materials on hand.

Truth be told, I was finally something more than the drunk wife of a trust-fund boozer, and being at school provided me with the space I hadn't realized I needed and the chance to fulfill a purpose larger than myself.

There was, however, a downside to my new world—summoning the strength to endure Wayne's bitter jabs. Whenever I shared something from my classroom day with him, he'd redirect the conversation to something unsavory from his own high school experience with resentment dripping from his words, such as, "I made it through four years of high school without reading 'Beowulf' and I turned out okay," or "I hope you don't hate any of your students like my English teacher hated me." He always found a way to twist even the smallest tidbit of the present into a self-centered negative experience from his past, but I never quipped back or stood up for myself.

Living under my mother's vicious tongue conditioned me to take the insults as they came rather than fight back, especially when alcohol could escalate any attempt to stand my ground. For my own peace of mind, I tightened my lips and sucked it up instead of reacting to his digs.

After dinner, I'd retire to the Smuggler's room for the night, where the silhouetted young writer captured in the mural who had such an urgent yet misguided hunger to write would haunt me. That was a few lifetimes and light years ago, though, when I was naïve, and both writing and the real Smuggler's Inlet provided me with the solace I needed. With my classroom now my refuge, I visualized the mural's notebook changing into a gradebook, just as the mural replaced the real Smuggler's since I hadn't so much as driven through the parking lot in months.

While I still struggled to transfer both my emotions and my existence onto the pages of my journal, writing about Shannon and our budding friendship came easily to me. I sensed in her an unspoken desire for something, but she gave me the impression of being so composed and collected, I couldn't imagine her life being devoid of anything. I revered her expertise in her craft and her innate knowledge of literature. She taught me more about "Beowulf" than I ever could have learned from a teaching guide. I thanked the universe for delivering me a mentor whose authenticity and infectious passion for both teaching and literature inspired me to my very core.

In place of staying late in my classroom or heading straight home on Friday afternoon, Waterville tradition rerouted my after-school destination to Delancy's, a quaint and trendy shore-themed bar and grill that opened on the Boulevard about four years ago. Thousands of white lights hung like garland over the bar's entrance and twinkled no matter the time of day or the season. A rush of warmth engulfed me as a group of teachers already assembled near the front hollered my name in unison when I walked in, which made me laugh. I made my way to the backside of the bar, where I saddled up next to Shannon and giggled, "I feel like I'm a cast member in a sitcom."

"You're right, we are a little like a group of

television barflies in greeting our Waterville fellows. Let me order you a seltzer, with lemon, right?"

"Thank you, a seltzer with lemon would be fantastic right about now."

I scanned the room to see who took part in the chorus of my greeting while Shannon ordered our drinks. A group of teachers I hadn't yet met but recognized from seeing in the halls were playing darts. Fellow English teachers Monica Moredachi and something DelVecchio, who apparently didn't have a first name because everyone called her Del, were piling their plates high at the free appetizer bar. Two male teachers dressed in gray gym shorts and black polo shirts with stitching underneath the Waterville Stingray logo identifying them as members of the physical education department were having an animated discussion with Al Myers, the weasel, and Rob Fields, the business teacher.

The comforting atmosphere created by the whitewashed-wood bar with its shiny brass rail, the innermost wall covered from floor to ceiling with antique surf culture tin signs and framed posters, and the company of my coworkers manifested a newfound sense of belonging inside me.

"Boy, that's some grin you've got going on there." Shannon handed me my seltzer, drank her whiskey in one swallow, and leaned in so I could hear her over the din of the bar. "It's a hoot to observe the interactions of our colleagues, and trust me, the scene can get quite interesting after a few drinks."

The pungent whiskey on Shannon's breath briefly teased me, but I resisted and took a satisfying drink from my seltzer. "Is Oliver coming?" I asked.

"No, he's got a late meeting and won't be home until

at least nine. Will Wayne be joining us?"

I fidgeted with my straw. "I kind of didn't tell him I was coming here."

"Understood." She subtly nodded to two teachers standing at the bar across from us. "Those two, they teach science."

"Are they science teachers or surfers? They both could have stepped out of a surf magazine, or a billboard for Stubby's Surf Shop."

"The one on the left is Phil Nice, and yes, he's nice. The other one, with the sandy hair and the round-framed glasses, not so much. He's the one I told you about, Dan Hampton."

My eyes widened. "You mean, the ex?"

"Yes, indeedy. Oh, shit…" Shannon squirmed in her chair as Dan ambled in our direction with two teeming shot glasses.

He gave her the cold shoulder and walked straight over to me, his raspy voice cracking. "I'm Dan. How was your first week in our Stingray pool?"

My attempt to play it cool failed, and I stammered like a simpleton. "I, um, I had a great first week. My students, they're pretty awesome."

Dan extended one of the glasses to me. "It's a Stingray tradition that all new teachers do a shot with me."

I raised my hand in front of me and said, "While I appreciate the gesture, I must decline with regret because I don't drink."

He furrowed his brow. "Never had anyone refuse a free shot before. I guess you're up then, Moran."

Shannon reluctantly accepted his offering, and they bent their heads back to empty their glasses. The air around us teemed with friction as Dan aimed to spark up a conversation. "So, what's new with you?"

Her gaze shifted between the restroom door and the vintage longboard suspended from the ceiling as she dryly replied, "Oh, you know, nothing much, same old, same old."

Dan was quiet for a moment, then he leaned in towards her and hissed, "How's that son of a bitch, Oliver?"

"For shit's sake, Dan." Shannon's voice increased in volume. "Here I thought you finally moved on, but once again, I'm wrong. Go away and leave me alone."

"Bitch." He skulked over to the court surrounding Al, who flailed his arms while arguing about something which was most likely of no consequence to anyone.

The crimson in Shannon's cheeks slowly faded. She summoned the bartender for a beer then said to me, "Thank God he's gone. Now, you owe me details, my friend. Going from a self-proclaimed party girl to an English teacher is not exactly a lateral career move."

Monica and Del came thundering over with Monica squawking, "Yes, tell us, please."

"Okay." I inhaled. "Here's the condensed version. After spending most of my days drunk as a skunk with my husband, an inclination to reclaim my life and go back to college awakened in me. I took a chance and applied to Sullivan University as a transfer student. To my surprise, they accepted me even with the 0.0 I earned while drunk for an entire semester at Gardner College."

Del's eyes enlarged. "A 0.0, you say? Impressive, in a bizarre kind of way."

I covered my face with my hands for a split second then continued, "Believe me, I'm not proud of failing by any means. My GPA at the end of my third semester at Gardner was a 3.5, but then I tanked my academic career by being tanked every single day. Anyway, fast forward a few years, I worked forty hours a week while attending Sullivan full time at night and on weekends. When I did my student teaching last semester, my boss allowed me to switch my schedule and report to work after my school day ended. I graduated in May, and here I am now, teaching with all of you at Waterville High School. I can't thank you enough for making me feel so welcome."

"We adore you, Kelly." Monica squealed and yanked me close to initiate an English department group hug.

Al weaseled up from behind and taunted, "So much love, unicorns, and glitter in you silly English teachers. Kelly, the harsh truth is teaching sucks. We are nothing but glorified babysitters, the parents despise us, and the kids are a bunch of degenerates. The best part about teaching is having summers off."

"Go away, Al. Teachers like you are the reason people hate us." Monica howled as Del pushed him back like a bouncer and sang like she was on stage, "There's no department like the English department," which ended up becoming a battle of the departments that migrated to the front of the bar.

"Al's such a douche," Shannon said after gulping what was left in her pint glass. "I respect the hell out of you, Kel, for having the guts to take a chance and redirect your life like you did. I wish I..." her voice trailed off and she frowned.

"You wish what?"

Shannon stilled for a moment, then shook her head back and forth. "Nothing. It's nothing. Just promise me you won't neglect the writer who is hibernating inside your soul. I see her lurking there. It's never too late to become the writer your younger self aspired to be."

****

The following week ushered in another milestone as a first-year teacher: my inaugural Back to School Night, the school's open house which provided parents a chance to meet their teenagers' teachers and experience the classrooms firsthand. Shannon and I stayed through from the end of the school day without going home in order to grade our students' "Beowulf" essays. When I wasn't sure what to do if a student's writing fell between levels on the assessment rubric, she advised, "Note the student's strength, and go up a number if you perceive extraordinary effort."

We finished grading at the same time after working for two hours straight, and Shannon melodramatically wiped her hand across her forehead. "Whew, we finished, at last."

"I never would have made a dent in this pile without you." I neatened my stack of essays.

"No problem. When I was a newbie, Connie Howard took me under her wing. She was one of the best teachers to ever grace these halls, very supportive and a real role model, and my retirement gift to her was my vow to be just as helpful to her replacement as she was to me. Have you reviewed the short story unit?"

I wrinkled my nose and answered in a forced monotone voice, "Yes, and I'm ready to go with Joyce's 'Araby.' "

"You still haven't lost your aversion to my very good friend, James Joyce."

"To be honest, the story itself wasn't atrocious, but

I didn't like how the last sentence contained the epiphany. The abrupt ending and lack of resolution left me hanging. I wanted more."

Shannon shook her head in mock derision, then gesticulated wildly. "But that's why Joyce is so relevant, even today. Real life is not glitter and puppies and pink fluffy goodness. Real life is messy. The epiphanies we experience, when we're suddenly hit in the face with an iron frying pan, especially the ones that hurt, the ones that dishearten and forever change us, that's real life. If you were mad at the ending, then Joyce did his job as a writer."

"Hmmm, I never thought about it as such. I did envy his use of imagery, his descriptions just flowed so naturally. I struggled with flowing imagery and action together when I used to write."

"See? Joyce is already making you reflect on yourself, so I'm proving my case. 'Araby' is from his collection of shorts titled *Dubliners*—" Her tone softened. "—and I'd give anything to travel to Dublin and see the places he wrote about with my own eyes."

"Why don't you?"

She shrugged and fiddled with the papers in front of her. "You know, we get like no time off. Oliver is too busy with work and I wouldn't want to go without him. I almost made it to Dublin during my sophomore year in college, but my father suffered a heart attack the day before I was supposed to leave. Talk about misfortune."

"Was he okay?"

"Yeah, he underwent a triple bypass, but you'd never know it by the number of 5 K races he enters. I told myself I'd make it to Dublin the following year, and so on, but the presumed next year just hasn't happened yet."

I perceived an intense yearning in Shannon's eyes, and I instinctively placed my hand on her shoulder. "Shan, it's clear you've got to do this. You're Irish, for God's sake, and you know more about James Joyce than anyone on this planet. You told me to remember my younger self who desired to write, right? Well, heed your own advice and go to Dublin this summer."

"Maybe. I always believed Dublin is where I'll find what's missing."

"What do you mean? What's missing?"

Shannon glimpsed wistfully out of the window at a V-shaped flock of birds flying south in the azure sky. When I understood she had no intention of answering me, I posed, "What are you waiting for? Make this dream of yours a reality."

She abruptly squeezed my hand for a mere second then she shook it off. "Enough of this. It's nothing but a silly bucket list item, anyway."

I thought it best to change the subject instead of prodding further, so I asked, "So, my captain, any last words of wisdom for my first Back to School Night?"

"You included the right talking points in your presentation. If someone requests information about his or her student specifically, tell them to arrange a conference appointment through the guidance office. You might be a new teacher, but you've got it where it counts and you'll do great, Kelly. Tonight, it's just a start and there's so many more events coming."

"Like what?"

"Like chaperoning the prom, for one." My face contorted into a grimace, and she asked, "You don't like prom?"

"I skipped my junior prom, but my senior prom was

downright awful. I didn't want to go at all, but my mother—" I rolled my eyes. "—you know the type of woman who wears a horrendous cheetah-print coat to impress people? That was her. She thought her reputation as a so-called successful mother would be ruined if I went to prom with a group of friends, that others would judge her because I couldn't find a date, so she forced me to go with her friend's horrible nephew. I'm pretty sure she paid him to take me, and she bought me the most sickening mess of a dress in the worst possible shade of bubblegum pink, complete with a gaudy rhinestone bow at the chest. I hated that horrible frock with a gut-wrenching passion."

I picked up a rogue pink marker resting on top of my desk, held it out for effect, then hurled it across the room into the garbage can.

"Nice shot."

"I didn't even know the guy, much less want to go to my prom with him. All she wanted was a framed prom portrait hanging on the living room wall to impress visitors. My illustrious date ended up drinking in the parking lot the whole evening with his idiot frat brothers who showed up out of nowhere, then he took off with one of the waitresses to God knows where. One of the worst nights of my life, but I got him back in the end."

Shannon bounced in place and squealed, "Oooh, what did you do?"

"His keys were in my purse, but I didn't know how to drive a stick shift so I walked home underneath lightning flashing in the distance and thunder starting to rumble. When I passed his car in the lot, I rolled down every window, then I threw his keys into the woods. The rain destroyed my hideous prom dress, but more importantly, it also short circuited the car's electrical system and ruined the leather interior." The crooks of my mouth bowed slightly up as the satisfaction of the small yet malicious, ill-conceived victory came to mind. "That dickhead deserved everything he got, and the suffering afterward I endured from my mother was totally worth it. She never got a portrait to frame, either."

Shannon's devilish smirk emulated mine and she growled, "Diabolical. I love it."

Del burst into the room with Monica at her heels yodeling, "I'm starving here. Where to for dinner, friends?"

After a short discussion, we decided to go to The Gutter, the new coffeehouse on the Boulevard a few doors down from Delancy's. I perused the menu once we were seated but there wasn't much to my liking, my finicky palate once again proving to be a nuisance to my hunger. When Scott the server took our order and I said, "Quesadillas and a water with lemon," Monica furrowed her brow.

"You ordered an appetizer. Wouldn't you rather have a salad or one of their balsamic-based signature sandwiches?" she suggested.

"Not really. To me, balsamic vinegar tastes how I think a quart of motor oil would taste. I'm fine with the quesadillas."

Del's bewildered face told me I might have come across too harshly, so I posed, "I know Shannon grew up in south Jersey and graduated from the University of Notre Dame, but I hardly know anything about either of you. Tell me something so I can get to know you better."

Always with a flair for the dramatic, Monica's face lit up and she sang, "Well, my hometown is Jacksonville,

Florida, and I left the sunshine state for The University of New Jersey after high school. Del and I met on our first day as Nighthawks."

"You two were acquainted before working at Waterville? I didn't know..."

"Yup," Del interrupted. "My girl here was my freshman year roommate. We lived together from our very first day of college until two years ago when this one tied the knot. Peter Moredachi was kind enough to let me rent the apartment above their garage, so we still share the same address but with a driveway between us."

"She's my bestie for sure." Monica nodded and put her arm around Del's shoulder. "Where did you grow up, Kelly?"

"Oldentown Beach," I murmured under my breath as I prepared for what I knew was coming.

Del jerked her head, gave me the evil eye, and started ranting, "No, you didn't just say that. Oldentown Beach, as in our rival, 'Oldentown Bitch?' You dirty, stinking Otter. The Stingrays will sting you." Del made zapping sounds interspersed with loud boos so much so the server came over and told her to keep it down. "You may be in college now, Scott, but I taught you for two years. You can't tell me what to do," she roared and pretended to pummel his stomach.

Monica and Del then headed to the restroom and Shannon confessed, "I love them both, but sometimes, they can be over the top. Based upon what you've told me, I assume your relationship with your mother isn't the best."

My face soured. "It's nonexistent. I haven't seen or talked to either of my parents in years. My father, what a miserable son of a bitch. He pretended I didn't exist most of the time, and the odd time he did get involved, he acted as her wingman in harassing me. My mother, I don't know..." Shannon's empathetic green irises coerced me to continue. "It's like I shamed her by being born. She was more into controlling me than being motherly. She's the reason I stopped writing. I keep in touch with my younger brother, Christian, though he's not so little anymore. He's twenty-four now and lives in Key West with his partner, Diego. My mother cut off all ties to him after he came out of the closet."

"Jeez." Shannon scowled. "How awful that someone could do such a thing to their own kid."

"They were really tight, too, and he was crushed when she was more concerned about how others would judge her for having a homosexual son rather than accepting him for who he is." I stared upward at a fan's chain shimmying in rhythm with its blades. "We were nothing but pawns to her and had no choice but to submit to her will."

I cleared my throat as I spotted Monica and Del on their way back to the table with Scott the server at their heels precariously carrying a balanced tray loaded with our dinner orders.

"Monica and Shannon, to our fourth Back to School Night, and, Kelly, to your first." Del raised her balsamic chicken sandwich into the air as a toast then she shifted the dinner discussion to a heated debate about whether Macbeth, Hamlet, or Othello would win in a bar fight.

My money was on Macbeth, no holds barred.

I danced to my car on an emotional high after Back to School Night ended. On the drive home, I thought about the mother who told me her son loves English this year because I tell stories, and she often finds him writing in his notebook when he used to only play video games.

Finding Wayne dead to the world and drooling on the couch, however, was the pin that deflated me. I stepped over the bottles on the floor and ventured to remember just what made him so alluring in the first place.

"His eyes. It was his eyes, and the beer, and a way out of that hellhole of a home," I whispered.

I stood up too fast, and once I steadied myself from the dizzying rush in my head, I retired to the Smuggler's room, where I relived my school day and night on the pages of my journal with unexpected fluency and a sense of pride.

My thoughts turned to Wayne and how he used to light up my world.

Was I wrong for wanting more out of life than what could be found inside of a keg or a bottle?

My soul, it used to be filled with words, but now it desired to inspire my students, to make a positive impact on their lives and help shape their futures.

In contrast, behind those sea glass blues that used to mesmerize me so, Wayne's soul contained nothing more than empty amber bottles and pint glasses, many with cobwebs, and maybe the latest technological gadget from Moira. For a fleeting second, I thought I could help him to discover his true purpose like I believed I had found mine, but that vision faded when my mind's common sense overpowered my heart's fancies.

My path was deviating from his, it was true, and had been for a long time.

I was stuck in limbo, but I wasn't quite ready to throw in the towel just yet.

I unwillingly accepted these certainties with a groan and a sniffle and did not fall asleep until after two in the morning.

****

I experienced several other firsts as an educator over the next few months, including parent conferences, homecoming and spirit week festivities, the end of marking period rush, and packing Thanksgiving food baskets for less fortunate Watertown families. I eagerly anticipated the weekly Friday meet ups at Delancy's because my relationship with my colleagues grew stronger with every passing visit.

The calendar flipping its page from November to December meant the highlight of the year for all Waterville High School staff and students had arrived— The Welcome Saturnalia WonderShow. The tradition featured comical performances by most of the teachers, secretaries, aides, custodians, and cafeteria workers on the Waterville staff. Even bus drivers and the town mayor, a Waterville High School alumnus, were known to make cameo appearances. The Show, as it was affectionately known, took place on the last day of school before winter break with every member of the student body in the audience. Shannon assumed directorial duties during her first year on staff, and I delighted to take part in the opening dance number, in the background of two musical numbers, and in a skit poking fun at the typical high school stereotypes.

Rehearsals, though, were brutal, and most nights between the first week of December and The Show's performance I arrived home after seven. Some coworkers complained about the long practice hours, but I didn't mind them at all. I was a part of something new, something meaningful and exciting. The Show joined everyone together to work toward the common goal of showing our students how much they meant to us by outshining the previous year's performance.

I still journaled every night, no matter how late I came home or how tired I felt. On the eve of The Show, I realized I hadn't seen or said two words to Wayne in over a week. He was now a regular at The Rip Tide with his buddy, Ed. I should have felt guilty about not seeing him, but I didn't.

The day of The Show arrived at long last, and I was like a firecracker ready to explode from the minute I woke up. The stage lights momentarily blinded me when the curtain opened to kick off The Show as I bumped my hips with Shannon's in rhythm to the latest hit song encouraging listeners to get their sexy on by a former boy-band prodigy. My adrenaline pumped from the flurry of moving from segment to segment, and I never felt more alive. I changed costumes from a stressed-out intellectual to a highly-caffeinated cheerleader in less than thirty seconds during the high school dance parody and ran smack into Del, who dragged me onstage while pretending to punch my head.

We were forced to stall the show when everyone, and I mean every person onstage, backstage, and in the audience, laughed so hard during the skit with teachers in the suspension room in place of students. The normally-reserved Phil Nice's uproarious impression of the foolish hall wanderer brought the house down—"I don't even know why I'm in here, man. Wandering is good for the soul, and they're stifling my independence. Gee whiz, man…"

Absolutely hysterical.

I sang as loud as I could, off key no doubt, during the traditional finale with my left arm around Shannon and my right one encircling Del, "We Wish You A Happy Saturnalia, and Iani Kalendai." We received such a monstrous ovation from the student audience we answered three curtain calls. Shannon beamed like I had never seen, and I was proud of her and how hard she worked to provide our students and fellow staff members scores of moments they would always remember.

After the black velvet curtain closed for the final time, a gleeful Stingray family circle swept me up in jubilant celebration. It didn't matter Al the weasel stood to my immediate right, I just grinned and giggled when he said, "Nice job, newbie."

When the circle dissolved and everyone peeled off in separate directions to change back into their regular clothes, I spied Shannon arguing with Dan near the stage door exit. She chucked the six long-stemmed red roses I supposed he gave her to the ground and stormed out, then Dan shuffled his feet down the stairs, through the auditorium, and out the rear door.

Shannon resurfaced by my side a few minutes later with a quivering lip and her hands balled into fists. "What an asshole. It's been over two years since I ended our relationship, and he still manages to manipulate me."

"What did he say to you?" I handed her a tissue.

"It doesn't matter. I should know better than to let him get into here." Shannon vehemently pointed to her forehead with her index finger. "He knows just what to say, and how to say it, to make me feel like complete shit. Why do I even try anymore?" She wiped the mascara streaks off her face with the tissue.

"Screw him, Shannon. You did a great job today to

create something special for everyone, and you have every reason to be proud of yourself. Don't let his bruised ego ruin this moment for you."

The right side of Shannon's mouth curled up. "I did do a good job, didn't I?"

"You sure did, my friend."

Shannon flung her arms around me. "You always say the right thing to brighten my spirits, Kel. Are you coming to Delancy's later? It's not Friday, but we always go there after dismissal on the day of The Show."

"Indubitably. I'll be there."

Our principal then ordered everyone back to their respective schedules to finish out one last period before embarking upon our much-anticipated winter break.

I arrived back to my classroom just as my students trickled in for the final class period of the calendar year in controlled yet festive chaos. "All right, everybody, calm down," I urged and fanned the air with my arms, then my gaze fell upon a small yet mounting pile of gifts and cards on my desk. "For me?" I blinked back tears. "I never expected…"

"You're awesome, Ms. L.," yelled Noralee, the most gregarious of my last period crew. "You're not making us learn today, are you? Open your presents."

"Wonderful idea, Noralee, and thank you, everyone." I proceeded to unwrap the cornucopia of holiday offerings, which included two peppermint scented candles, a box of chocolate candy, five lottery scratchers, a tin of butter cookies, and a tree ornament with "Best Teacher" written on a blackboard.

When I picked up a red envelope with a cute little Santa sticker on it, the quietest student in the class named Martin caught my hand. "Please, Ms. Lynch, open mine later," he whispered.

"Sure thing, Martin. I appreciate you thinking of me," I replied, and he shuffled back to his desk.

I addressed the class. "So, with twenty minutes left, what should we do?"

"Tell us a story about your best Christmas ever," Noralee suggested, which was followed by a chorus of echoes, "Tell us."

"Okay." I nodded while gripping the lectern tight. I couldn't admit to my students I never experienced a memorable Christmas. Rather than make myself a target of pity, I did what I used to do best—I created a story on the spot.

"Gather round, friends." I swept my arms in the air and my students inched their desks closer. "I'll title this story 'The Imperfect Present.' When I was nine years old, I asked Santa for what everyone else in my class wanted."

Noralee asked, "What was it?"

"Some sort of new game system. I wasn't really into video games, but my classmates talked about all types of games they could play on this gray, handheld thing with red buttons and a little square screen. When I woke up on Christmas morning, I scampered to the living room. I guessed how big the box should have been and scoured every present's tag for my name, but I couldn't find one in such a size. I knew Santa visited, because all that remained from the cookies and milk I put out for him before I went to bed were a plateful of crumbs and an empty glass with a dried white ring inside its bottom. But what I wanted the most wasn't under my tree."

The classroom filled with rancorous exclamations of disbelief.

"You ended up getting it, right?" wondered Noralee.

"No." I shook my head. "I didn't."

"But...that's not fair."

I held the captive attention of every student in the room and took pleasure in the suspenseful sensation of anticipation I created. "Precisely. I said the same thing to myself, it wasn't fair. My parents came downstairs and found me weeping. When my Dad asked me what was wrong, I sobbed, 'I don't see a video game box for me.' My mom pointed out, 'But Santa left so many other gifts for you, Kelly.'

"And she was right. I did receive a lot of presents: clothes and a new teddy bear and an art set, but I wanted that gaming system so bad. Or so I thought. I'll never forget the last present I opened, a journal and pen set in my favorite colors, turquoise and purple. The journal was so pretty and glittery, with five sections filled with colorful paper and tons of stickers in a zippered pouch inside, and the pens even wrote in shimmering metallic ink. Santa left a note for me inside the journal telling me I could go anywhere and do anything by writing my own stories, and I could create my own characters instead of being a character inside of a game. Truth is, I never really wanted the game console, I only thought I did because everyone else did. But Santa gave me what I needed. That present, the one I didn't realize I wanted, was the best Christmas present I ever received, and I've been writing ever since."

"I'd be pissed I didn't get the game," Noralee grumbled, with a few other students nodding in agreement.

"Sometimes life teaches us the most valuable lessons when we don't receive what we most yearn for, and those lessons can shift the course of our lives for the better."

There was a row with students yelling their thoughts on the subject when someone abruptly shouted, "Whoa, whoa, whoa," from the back of the room. The quiet Martin rose from his seat with all eyes on him.

"Like in 'Araby,' the boy let his disappointment ruin his life, but his epiphany, it's part of his story. If Ms. Lynch got the game, she wouldn't be telling us this story. She started writing because of that journal."

The dismissal bell screaming from the speaker shattered the classroom's pervading silence. My students jostled to the door while I hollered, "Have a great break and make smart decisions. I want to see you all back here next year."

Once the room emptied, I wrote on a blue sticky note, "Martin…epiphany…my story…the silence and anticipation…should I write again?"

Then it dawned on me that Shannon had been correct. A mere snippet of James Joyce's inspiration left a positive imprint on both Martin and me, and my heart galloped in elation.

****

Monica's voice resounded off the hallway lockers as she yodeled "Delancy's Time" to the tune of "O Tannenbaum," so I stored what I needed to grade over break in my satchel, flicked the light switches to the off position, and whispered, "Merry Christmas. See you next year," to the classroom ghosts before I closed the door.

The festive air of The Show transcended to Delancy's with circles of camaraderie as far as the eye could see, and the perceptible absence of both Dan and

Al made it all the more delightful. If I could have, I would have captured the jubilance in a bottle and taken it home with me. I danced a few steps with Del, who passed me on to Monica, who yodeled the lyrics to every song sounding through the speakers. I made my way to Shannon, who perched on a barstool in our usual spot at the back of the bar, glad she put the earlier unpleasantries with Dan aside. "Hey, you." She gleamed. "Is today the greatest, or what?"

"It sure is. I'm too excited to sit. I can't remember the last time I felt this…" I could not find the words to describe the soothing warmth spinning inside every cell of my being. My gaze connected with hers and I sputtered, "I'm…I'm…I'm actually at a loss for words. This merry, I guess?"

"Speaking of merry—" She reached into her purse and handed me a present covered with shimmering silver and red paper. "—this is for you. Open it later."

My mouth dropped open and my cheekbones burned. "We discussed this, Shan, about not getting gifts for each other, that everything was too hectic with The Show. I am a gigantic ass for not getting you anything." I hung my head while clutching her impeccably wrapped package.

"Kelly, your friendship is your gift and I couldn't ask for anything more. But there is something you can do for me in place of an actual present."

I straightened my spine. "Anything. You name it."

"Really think about what I wrote inside your gift. I may have only known you for a few months, but you are better than your situation and bigger than Waterville."

"What do you mean?"

"You'll figure it out someday."

I placed the present inside my purse with sublime gratification filling me from head to toe and asked, "What are your plans over break?"

"We're spending Christmas Eve at my aunt's house, then playing it by ear because Oliver will probably have to travel up to Boston for business. If he does, I'll tag along with him and read or wander around Beantown while he's working. How about you?"

"Nothing. It's always just the two of us because Wayne's mother heads to South Beach a week or so after Thanksgiving, and with my brother in Florida, we don't have any other family."

"Want to come to my aunt's place for Christmas Eve, you and Wayne?"

"I appreciate the offer, but we're good."

Shannon slung her arm at my waist and tugged me close. "If Oliver's plans change, I'll give you a ring, but I think you'll find my present will keep you very busy over break."

"Oh, really?" I smirked. "I can't wait to see what you gave me."

Del sauntered toward us with her flashing Christmas light necklace almost blinding me. She sang along with the rock-version rendition of a song about Santa Claus resonating through the speakers. At Del's insistence, Shannon and I cavorted up to the front with her to join our Stingray family arm in arm, and all was right with the world.

****

I fired through the front door of our townhouse later that afternoon like a rocket, forgetting I hadn't seen my husband in days.

"Wayne? Are you here?" I enthusiastically called as

I hung my school satchel on its hook. I checked the
room, the bedroom, and the bathroom, but couldn't
him. The empty beer cans in the kitchen tipped me o
Wayne was out with Ed.

So be it.

Instead of holing up in the Smuggler's room, I
grabbed my laptop along with Martin's card and
Shannon's gift and locked the door behind me. The
monster cold stung my face while I trudged back to the
parking garage, but it failed to chill me because the day's
inebriation of satisfaction kept me warm. I headed to The
Gutter for a latte then continued on the route I knew as
well as the back of my hand but hadn't traveled since last
winter.

I navigated through the abandoned Smuggler's Inlet
parking lot and pulled into the spot nearest the sea. After
sitting in solitude for a few moments, I ran my finger
underneath the sealed triangle on the back of Martin's
red envelope.

Inside was a simple greeting card with a snowman
feeding a cardinal from his hat. This card wasn't from a
box of stock holiday cards, though, but purchased
individually from a store display. I opened to a
handwritten greeting in pencil on white lined paper taped
over its pre-printed tiding—

Dear Ms. L,

I hated English class every year until this year. I am glad you are my teacher because I like how you tell stories to go along with what we are learning. My secret is I've always loved to write, and because of your help, I am getting better at it. That story by James Joyce, I get that kid, and in the past, I let life piss me off like he did. Not anymore. Life is life, whether something good bad. *The point is getting through* help *for me to do that.*

I actually made a difference.

Martin's letter validated the three versions of me in existence: me the person, me the writer, and me the teacher. The true triple whammy of reassurance sparked my light, which was shining brighter than ever.

I fixated my gaze on the incoming tide and thought about the yarn I spun for my class about getting the journal set for Christmas and what Martin said afterward.

That nonexistent journal was the best gift I never received.

I set Martin's card aside and tore the beautiful paper from Shannon's present to reveal a brand new copy of *The Portrait of an Artist as a Young Man* by James Joyce.

"Of course, it is." I chuckled before reading Shannon's inscription inside the front cover:

Kelly,

You are a great teacher, but I see the writer behind your eyes. You don't know where to start? Start like Joyce did. Just sit down and write. Once you write chapter one, everything will fall into place. Don't deny your calling. "I mean, said Stephen, that I was not myself as I am now, as I had to become." James Joyce, Portrait. *Like Stephen, you are not yourself as you are now, as you have to become. This moment is everything. Follow the light and trust the journey as you move forward toward your true purpose.*

With gratitude and love,

Your friend always,
Shannon

The green flag waved for a new set of soggy tears to race from my eyes.

Shannon's message stunned me.

How could she see the real me underneath the teacher mask I wore, when I couldn't see her myself? I denied her existence ever since the hands of my mother destroyed my words. Fate united Shannon and I as coworkers a few months ago, but it felt like I had known her forever.

She encouraged me to write.

Encouragement, from someone who cared about me.

Imagine that.

I cradled the book in my hands and closed my eyes, quietly existing in the present moment. All at once, I craved to feel alive, so I departed my car and strode along the inlet's wall toward the ocean with the northeast wind blowing wildly through my hair and the waves spraying the rocks below me.

I closed my eyes as remnants of that haunting evening at this exact spot came flooding into my memory…

It was my first night home from Gardner College after earning the 0.0 by ditching my classes to drink the semester away. One morning near the semester's end, I returned to my dorm room after an all-night bender with my face covered in dirt, my hair matted with leaves and twigs, the corners of my mouth teeming with dried-up funk, and my panties wet from what I hoped was passing out in a puddle but most likely from something else. I opened the door to find all of my roommate's belongings gone and a scathing note on my bed informing me the last random drunk I brought home broke into her lockbox and stole her jewelry and a hundred dollars in cash. Crushed by guilt, I crumbled on Taryn's barren bed and bawled my eyes out.

I never thought I could hate myself more than I did in that moment, but I was wrong.

The day I came home a Gardner failure topped it, with bells on.

I took shelter in my room and had just finished another round of crying when my mother summoned me like a dog by screaming my name. I inched down the stairs, rounded the corner from the living room to the kitchen, and raised my head to find her clasping a torn envelope addressed to me from Gardner in her left hand and my semester grade sheet in her right. The most vicious scowl I had ever seen on her face vibrated across her cheekbones.

She didn't say a word but punched me in my right cheek without warning. I lost my balance and literally saw stars when my tailbone slammed upon the hard floor with a thump. Then came the shriek at the top of her lungs, "This was supposed to be a 4.0, not a 0.0!"

My father cowardly stood with his back against the wall as I cowered in disgrace, a witness to her frenzy instead of intervening to help or defend me.

"How am I ever going to explain this to everyone?" She continued ranting, "How could that school let this happen without notifying me?" She gave me another backhand across my left cheek. "If you intend on living under this roof, you better wake up bright and early tomorrow to find a job to pay back the money you've wasted. Otherwise, get the hell out of this house!"

Enduring the Waves

I stumbled to my feet amid the condemnation and expletives and hurried to my room, where the blood flowing from my nose saturated too many tissues to count. I panted and sobbed so hard I ended up dry heaving, which made my fresh facial bruises throb with even more pain.

I dreaded that moment for months and expected the hostility, but I never fathomed I'd experience such an insane level of violence or to feel so immensely insignificant.

I had no place to go, nobody to ask for help, and was trapped in that devil's den of shame and judgment. I burrowed under my blanket, devastated and beaten, and didn't move for hours.

Near midnight, long after I cried myself dry and everyone else in the house was asleep, I jammed my turquoise stuffed dolphin into my backpack and snuck out of the house. I shuffled with slumped shoulders along the route I had traveled a thousand times with a trickle of stars lighting my way. Before long, the song of the waves rhythmically lapping against the sea wall shattered the silence between my ears.

Smuggler's was nearly deserted except for a few teens gathered near the parking area. The fog horn at the end of the south jetty bellowed its song to guide the seafarers home just as a fishing vessel entered the inlet with its outstretched outriggers raising to form a "V" over the boat. The "Tracey Lynn," an out-of-area vessel from Beauford, South Carolina, listed past me with its anchors and chains clanging on its way to the offload docks.

I scaled the rocks, oblivious at first to the gossamer crescent moon's glittering reflections upon the water, as the air's droplets dampened my hair. Once I came to the spot where I used to write, I yanked the dolphin from my backpack and ripped open the seam along its belly, which caused its billowy stuffing to blow in every direction. I carefully dissected a blue bottle from its innards then threw the furry carcass into the tide.

Nobody else knew the bottle existed.

Besides writing, another way I coped with my mother's relentless cruelty over the years was by purchasing small packages of sleeping pills from the local pharmacy. This was before there were any age restrictions to buy such products, and I bought them so infrequently I didn't raise any red flags with the store clerks. Once I got home, I'd transfer the pills into the blue bottle then discard the packaging inside an empty tampon box. Roughly eight pharmacy trips over the years yielded almost two hundred sleeping pills in the bottle.

I never actually considered taking the pills as a viable option, until then.

What other choice did I have?

The little blue bottle contained the ultimate salvation from my eternal failures and unending humiliation and was the solution to the inevitable day when I could take no more.

"That day…is…today," I whimpered to the heavens.

I poured about a third of the pills into my left hand and clutched them tight in anguish with my chest pounding, the overwhelming impulse to follow through with the next step creeping ever closer to becoming a reality.

I should have never been born.

A lone tear escaped my eye, rolled down my left cheek, and landed on my hand clasping the pills. A stinging coolness spread along the tear's trail while the eastward gusts struck my face.

No more moving forward.

No more chasing the non-existent light like an idiot.

It was a farce.

What had I discovered from my mistakes?

I.

Was.

Nothing.

A car circled through the lot on the Glenharbor side of the inlet, and when it parked, its headlights subtly illuminated me from a distance.

The light.

I quavered, and an impalpable force drew my focus to the blinking red light atop the fog horn.

Stop.

Stop how?

I gradually comprehended the absolute finality of the moment and my entire being burned white hot. I shifted my gaze from the red light to my clenched hand which trembled vehemently.

"No!" I cried out and flung the handful of pills followed by the blue bottle into the inlet's outgoing current…

I never told anyone about what happened that night, not even Wayne.

I stood steadfast and lucid in the present moment with the changing tides in front of me.

Shannon.

Martin.

My words.

Three of the reasons I did not succumb to my demons on that agonizing evening.

I inhaled the salt air deep to purify my lungs, opened my eyes, and spanned the scene in front of me before scrambling toward the flat rock extending into the water.

Intense chills spread over my entire body like a spilled bucket of ice water the moment I stepped onto it. The ghost of my former self, the writer hidden deep within my soul, stirred as my silhouette in the Smuggler's mural roused.

"Okay, I…I…I get it," I stammered as I caught sight of a trawler coming into sight just on the horizon.

Coming home through the light.

I fondled the triskele in my pocket.

My words.

My soul.

My light.

I stridently marched back to my car, and with the foghorn's song the soundtrack to my moment of everything, I powered on my laptop and feverishly wrote for hours.

Chapter Two

"I'm Kay. He's Ess. We fight as one for what's right. Today we learned a restaurant fills a small dumpster with their leftover food at the end of each night. We are traveling to Big Bell's Kitchen in The Big Apple's Hell's Kitchen on a mission to persuade the restaurant owner to donate the leftovers to the homeless shelter on the next block full of teens like us who are hungry and require nourishment..."

More than a decade had passed since I last scripted the antics of Kay and Ess, the dynamic duo I created when my notebook was my closest companion. My favorite stories to write when I was younger were about two best friends I dubbed "The Benevolenters." I molded the main character, a female named Kay, into a much braver version of me. She stood up for both herself and the downtrodden in a world where doubt and shame didn't exist. She had the best sidekick ever, a clever male named Ess who sported a husky build and gentle brown irises with flecks of gold near his pupils. Together, they embarked upon adventure after adventure in their pursuit to help those in need, especially young underdogs like me, and right the wrongs in society.

Inspired by the day's gifts of purpose and insight, a viable first draft of a Benevolenters episode came to life through my fingers as I wrote in front of Smuggler's with my car protecting me from the early winter gale. The final word appeared on my screen just as fiery reds and oranges blazed above me. My mind wandered to a different blaze with roaring and lethal flames intentionally set by my mother's hands which murdered my writing, including every Benevolenters story I ever scripted prior to today.

The sky's fire faded into watery purples and blues, and I headed home after the last slice of color disappeared. Ideas flooded my mind, though, and my drive took twice as long as usual because I kept pulling over to scribble them down. A phenomenon of exhilaration fueled the embers of something still smoldering deep within my soul.

Wayne's coat and sneakers carelessly strewn on the floor in the middle of the hall slightly subdued my elation. "Wayne? Where are you?" Muffled groans resonated from the back bedroom, so I grabbed a bottle of water from the refrigerator and gently beckoned into the room, "Wayne? You okay?"

"What? Who there?" He befuddled and bolted upright.

"It's just me. I brought you some water."

I cracked the bottle's seal open and waited for him to stop grinding the palms of his hands into his eye sockets. His squinty eyes gradually revealed more of their spellbinding blue hue as he chugged the water. When the bottle was empty, he grunted, "You bring dinner?"

"I've got a pot of water warming up on the stove for pasta, and another one simmering with sauce and those little meatballs you love."

"Not Antonio's, but still good. I'm starving." He staggered down the hall to the kitchen and swigged down a beer before dropping onto the couch.

A running list of things I hoped to discuss with Wayne formed, so I stirred the sauce with one hand and jotted a tally with the other. Wayne wrestled with navigating the channels on the remote and paused on a corny holiday commercial. Red and green lights surrounded white automobiles and flashed in tempo with a hackneyed remake of a holiday classic, implying a brand new vehicle topped with an immense, red bow was preferable to peace on earth.

Holy crap.

I never decorated for Christmas.

What was the matter with me?

My scarlet hot cheeks were probably the same tint and temperature as the bubbling sauce on the stove.

I dished out the pasta and meatballs onto the garish dinner plates gifted to us after our wedding by an associate of Moira's while cringing from both the gaudy floral pattern on the china dinnerware and my forgetfulness. Wayne balanced his plate on his stomach after I handed it to him, the hockey game on television consuming his half-sober attention, and he ended up dropping more of his meal on his bare chest than he disgustingly slurped in between guzzles of beer.

I withdrew to the kitchen riding a wave of nausea. I scraped my plate into the trash can, then hurried down the hall and made it to the bathroom just in time to toss the little amount I had eaten into the toilet.

****

With sleep still swimming in my eyes, I embarked on a predawn mission to right my faux pas and welcome seasonal joy into the townhouse. Thankfully, Wayne had drifted back to the bedroom at some point last night, and

I transformed the empty living room into a scene of coastal Christmas in record time. The colossal starfish Santa from Moira radiated holiday cheer from the middle of the wall with our cream-colored velvety stockings symmetrically placed on either side of it. I outlined the room with white twinkle lights, then I overlaid shells and sea glass on ornament hooks to hang like icicles. Every beachy holiday knickknack I amassed over the years found a home throughout the living space. I thought about keeping the green sea glass Christmas tree, with its mermaid topper and fairy lights weaved in between every delicate glass branch, in the Smuggler's room, but the handcrafted decoration belonged as the focal point of the living room so I placed it in the center of the coffee table.

When I finished, I fixed myself a mug of peppermint coffee and nestled into the sofa.

The minty elixir and the satisfaction of creating the festive atmosphere warmed my insides, but the short-lived sensation ended when Wayne straggled in, still groggy and wearing nothing but boxer shorts.

"Morning." He grunted while stretching then glanced at me through his squinty eyes. "Why aren't you holed up in the Smuggler's room doing whatever it is you do in there?"

"Just thought I'd admire my handiwork."

"Oh." He yawned and headed to the bathroom, scratching his ass the entire way.

My hint fizzled, and I considered I might be the one who was the ass here. My trembling hands created a wake in my coffee mug and I winced at the glaring reality of our deteriorated farce of a marriage. I could hear Shannon's encouraging voice between my ears, "Hey, you. It's time. You've got this."

I doubted I did.

Wayne flopped onto the sofa, and as he reached for the remote, I released my breath and took the plunge.

"Wayne, can we talk before you click on the television?"

"About what?"

"Us."

He groaned and let out a forced, over-the-top sigh. "Why now? I'm still asleep."

"Because I can't live like this anymore."

"Yeah," he sneered, "like you have it so bad."

I clenched my jaw. "What the hell is that supposed to mean?"

Wayne's irises grayed and he gritted his teeth before snapping, "Dammit, Kelly, I let you go back to college, and even though I pay your bills, I let you work a job where you stay late and bring home so much work that you're never finished. I don't demand sex from you, I let you sleep in your own room, and I stay out of your way. What more do you want from me?"

"I…I…" I stammered in disbelief as a ball of fire festered in my stomach. "What? You let me go back to college and work? Wayne, what about us? You and me?"

"That's rich, you and me. More like you and you."

My body stiffened. "I love my job, and I'm grateful we don't have to worry about money. But there's something missing. I miss the intimacy from when we first met tremendously."

"No, you don't," he roared. "It used to be great because we were both drunk and didn't give a shit about anything. Once you started with this nonsense of improving yourself, you became boring and bland." He sprang to his feet with menacing eyes. "You say you want that part of your life back? Well, I want my wife back, the woman I married who was fun and always up for a good time. Nothing like decorating for Christmas two days before it."

An unfamiliar sensation mounted from my stomach's fireball and shot up through my throat and out the top of my head. I fired back, "You could have decorated for Christmas too, you know, if you were so bothered by it, and your inheritance pays the bills, not you. What's so wrong with wanting more out of life? I am already making a difference at school, I'm writing again, and everything excites me. If you doubt me, read this from one of my students." I flung Martin's card at him. "While you are busy drinking your days away, I'm helping my students to be their best selves. I encourage them, I nurture their creativity, I…don't you want more out of life?"

Wayne hurled Martin's letter back at me without opening it and stomped his foot so hard the starfish Santa on the wall almost jumped off its hook. "I don't give a damn about what your student wrote. I don't have dreams or goals, I don't want to travel or see new places, and I'm okay with my life the way it is."

"But…"

"It's obvious I'm not good enough for you anymore, so I drink with Ed and the guys down at The Rip Tide. What part don't you understand?"

I froze as the hot fire inside of me recoiled into cold shame, and I couldn't prevent myself from sniveling. I faltered, "I'm sorry…me…teaching…writing…I just wish…" I swabbed my tears with the sleeve of my hoodie but they were soon too plentiful, so I buried my head into my arms.

I was human, and yes, I caved.

After a few minutes of letting me cry it out, Wayne sat down next to me and his voice softened. "Kel, we don't have it so bad. Let me have my life like I let you live yours."

He caressed my cheek then tilted my chin toward his. Our eyes locked, and those blasted sea glass irises of his worked their magic and rendered me helpless. He angled his mouth toward mine and kissed me with the same passion that scorched so long ago.

His spell still enchanted me.

I succumbed to the smoldering fervor aching in my loins and tugged him closer. My eager tongue explored his mouth. Tantalized, I hungered for more, more of him. I ripped off his boxers, he yanked down my sweatpants and we rolled onto the floor like the very first time we made love. I forgot about everything else as he thrusted on top of me, inside me, and I screamed in sheer ecstasy as I climaxed over and over.

His eyes still filled me with a rapture like no other, and I still loved him.

Wayne and I laughed like children later in the afternoon while selecting a perfectly scrawny tree from the ten misfits remaining at the last lot in Watertown with evergreens still available. We decorated our scraggly tannenbaum retro style by draping strands of multicolored lights with those giant, fat bulbs almost too heavy for the tree's limp branches and the gaudiest star topper we could find. I hung the handful of hand-me-down ornaments from the box in the attic and sprinkled handfuls of tinsel over it like confetti.

We ordered a pizza delivery from Antonio's, and

Wayne opted to imbibe his nightly booze fix at home rather than go to The Rip Tide. He fell asleep within the first few minutes of my favorite holiday movie featuring a house overly decorated with twinkle lights and a bumpkin cousin living out of a tenement on wheels. I covered him with a blanket, and he kicked it so violently it plummeted to the floor.

I left it where it fell.

A fiery force once again stirred inside me, one I denied and attempted to smother. I refuted its existence and skulked to the Smuggler's room with prickles running underneath the skin on my arms and legs.

In all reality, it did exist.

The truth in spades ridiculed me from the depths of my soul, but my heart still believed in fairy tales.

I wished for a miracle that night, but I never heard Santa's sleigh bells jingling in the yuletide sky.

****

Christmas morning arrived without fanfare or magic, and I stared at the sparkling lights in the Smuggler's ceiling while wishing away both the burning ball in my stomach and the grogginess from very little sleep. Once I heard Wayne stirring, I threw off my covers and wandered out to the living room with determination to make the magic happen. I was the author of my own story, dammit, and I wanted to be happy, even if such happiness was a mammoth lie and merely camouflaging the truth.

"Merry Christmas," he murmured in his sultry voice. His blues beamed when they connected with mine and enchantment lit up the air like invisible fireworks.

A playful grin rose from the corners of my mouth as I latched my fingers together behind his waist. "Merry

Christmas, yourself," I purred into his ear before our mouths connected. We fell to the floor in another fit of rapture, the euphoria of my rhythm in time with his, a seventh heaven on earth.

After leaving me heaving and satisfied on the carpet, he chuckled. "I kind of feel guilty ravishing you like that on the morning Baby Jesus was born."

"Yeah, but he was all about loving one another, so I think we're okay. We've got a legal document making such an act a requirement of our union, don't we?" I giggled as he tousled my hair and tickled my side.

"Want breakfast?"

"One of your sandwiches would be wonderful." Time froze as I got lost in his crystal blues, then he rustled and rose to his feet. I grabbed the blanket off the sofa to cover myself and remained sprawled on the floor while the glistening tinsel on the tree mesmerized me.

As Wayne busied himself in the kitchen, my mind's hamster raced at top speed in his wheel while spewing at the top of his lungs everything that was wrong with what just happened. No matter how much the damn hamster may have been correct, I didn't want to hear it. I jammed an invisible stick in the spokes of his wheel. He tumbled and quieted, but I couldn't entirely shake the sting from his reprimands.

After breakfast, we showered then exchanged gifts. Wayne surprised me with a new laptop, and I gave him the holiday season's hot ticket item—the latest game console featuring motion-controlled gaming. While wrapping it, I reminisced about the story I devised on the spot about the hand-held game system I never even received from Santa.

My students bought my story lock, stock, and barrel.

I could certainly spin the yarn to knit one hell of a tale.

Christian telephoned midafternoon, and in the middle of our conversation, he blurted out, "So, Dad kicked Mom to the curb last week."

"What?" I yelled so loud Wayne came thundering into the room.

"I thought you'd like that."

"You've got to be kidding."

Wayne furrowed his brow and waved his hands in the air so I mouthed the word "parents."

"The old man couldn't take her anymore. She moved in with that bitch friend of hers, Charlene. Dad says the divorce should be final by summer."

"Divorce?"—I squirmed in my seat—"holy shit, Christian, I can't believe this. I wonder what made him snap?"

"I don't know. He's mentioned several times in passing about being tired of looking and feeling like a fool, but something must have happened for him to break like this."

"Have you talked to her at all?"

Christian's voice raised. "Hell, no. You know I'll never speak to her again."

"Me either."

"You and I are the last bit of family we have, Kel, and I sure miss you. Maybe you can come down here sometime to visit."

"Maybe." An orb of discomfort churned in my tummy as I lied. "Or you guys could come up here?"

"Maybe." A like dishonesty trickled from his words. "Merry Christmas, Kelly."

"Merry Christmas, Christian. I love you, brother."

"I love you, too." His voice quavered before he hung up.

I sat there overflowing with both a longing to hug my brother and disbelief about my father standing up to that atrocious woman. In a twisted and sick kind of way, my wish for a Christmas miracle had been granted.

****

Wayne and I did something together almost every day despite his hangovers. Our holiday week-off bucket list included an excursion on the train to New York City to visit the legendary Rockefeller Center tree along with a gazillion other people, a walk in Sandy Point Park with snowflakes delicately floating down from above, and an afternoon jaunt to the Sullivan College Planetarium for their celestial new year's extravaganza. He still went to The Rip Tide with Ed every night, but he wasn't coming home as late or as sloshed.

In my downtime, I wrote.

And I wrote and wrote.

You get the idea.

I forgot how healing and fulfilling releasing words onto a paper or a screen felt, and I let them stream out like high tide screams into Smuggler's. I revised the draft Benevolenters episode featuring Kay and Ess's escapades to aid homeless teens in New York City, then I signed out a few library books to research the city's landscape. I wanted to make my story better by establishing an authentic setting while seeing if there was anything in the real Hell's Kitchen which might assist the duo in completing their humanitarian missions.

Nighttime was my personal writing time, when I'd allow my consciousness to stream onto the pages in front of me in Joyce-like fashion while paying no mind to sentence structure, spelling, or form. I titled one such anecdote about my college roommate "An Apology for Taryn," which was the most therapeutic piece I composed all week.

My voice was on point and my creativity rejuvenated.

I also held true to my promise to Shannon by reading *Portrait* in its entirety.

"You're reading Joyce?" Wayne scoffed when he caught the name on the book's cover.

"Shannon gave the book to me for Christmas. It's better than I expected."

"Why are there so many flags sticking out of it? It reminds me of a kaleidoscope fan."

"This is what my students do. They annotate and take notes while reading to have a more meaningful interaction with the literature."

"Blimey, seems like too much work for me. What happened to the idea of reading just to read?" Wayne balked and responded in a superbly awful British accent. "Don't plan on dragging me to any foo-foo book events or Shakespeare festivals, please."

"Don't worry, babe," I smirked. "Those are the last places I'd ever take you."

On the blustery eve of New Year's Eve, after Wayne and I lunched at Antonio's, I ventured out to The Gutter for my usual latte then read the fourth chapter in my car at Smuggler's.

"On and on and on and on he strode, far out over the sands, singing wildly to the sea, crying to greet the advent of the life that had cried to him." I read loudly after silently reading it twice and slapping two sticky flags on the page.

Here the mundane Stephen Dedalus, protagonist of *Portrait*, sang to the sea to celebrate his rebirth.

I flipped to the inside cover and read again what Shannon wrote. "Become myself…trust the journey as I become myself."

I shifted my gaze inward and my soul roused with an awakening as a gleaming new year dangled just upon the threshold. My education led to my current occupation, but words and stories were the continuous threads laced throughout my life's tapestry, including those that were disavowed, destroyed, or still in hiding. Goosebumps raced over my skin, and I basked in authenticity while symbolically singing to the sea's outgoing current gushing past me just as Stephen had done.

Almost as if the universe scripted it, I finished reading *Portrait* with seven hours left in the year while Wayne and Ed provided commentary for a college bowl game in the living room. After I read the last page, I understood why Shannon gave me the book.

"Welcome, O Life!"

I dialed her number but the call went straight to voicemail. "Hey, Shan, sorry I missed you. I finished *Portrait.* Thank you for believing in me. Be safe tonight and Happy New Year."

Welcome, O Words!

I lost myself in writing and didn't hear Ed cheering an interception by Miami in the final minute of the game to seal their victory over some team from Nevada, nor did I hear Wayne hollering for me to get ready.

"Kelly!" he yelled as he barged into the Smuggler's room.

I nearly threw my new laptop into the air. "Jesus,

Wayne. You scared the crap out of me."

"Let's go, hon. Time's a wasting." He tapped his finger on his wristwatch. "You said we'd go when the game's over, and it's over."

"All right, all right"—I muttered while saving my document—"I'm coming."

While I wouldn't have minded bypassing the revelries, getting dolled up for once did feel good. I slinked into a stylish yet comfortable long black dress with crocheted arms, curled my hair framing my face, and completed my preparation ritual with a simple application of mascara.

Wayne's gaze dipped when I twirled into the living room. "Now, there's the girl I married. You sure you don't want to do a pregame shot with us?"

"Yeah, Kelly," Ed reiterated Wayne's offer. "It is New Year's Eve, after all."

I shook my head and scolded, "You already know my answer, boys. Plus, I'm the designated driver for tonight's festivities. I wouldn't mind just hanging here, you know."

Wayne and Ed tossed back their shots, oblivious to my suggestion, then Ed gestured toward the window. "Check it out, it's snowing. I'm glad we're driving and not walking."

"You got that right," Wayne said, "and tonight we have our very own chauffeur. Miss Kelleeee, oh Miss Kelleeee, the new year is less than two hours away. Take us to The Rip Tide at once, dear."

When Ed yanked open The Rip Tide's door, the stench of muggy swill and the band's drunken cacophony walloped me right in my face. Wayne took my hand and threaded me through the partygoers to the center bar, where he ordered a triple whiskey with a beer chaser for both himself and Ed. I frowned as he incoherently yelled to me, his voice drowned out by the racket.

"What?" I screamed.

He just smiled at me.

The clamor combined with the stifling heat, the stink of stale booze, and the unfamiliar wall of shoulders encompassing me produced a disturbing trepidation inside me. The apprehension's weight increased second by second, and when it became too heavy to bear, I lost my composure and shouted into Wayne's ear, "I've got to get out of here!"

I elbowed my way through the crowd, barged through the door back into the cold, and plopped on an empty bench alongside The Rip Tide's building.

The chilly draft soothed my sweating forehead. I cradled myself with my crossed arms and rocked back and forth, slowly regrouping from the panicked claustrophobia and the unanticipated flashbacks to my inebriated prior persona.

Wayne sat down next to me after my panting and pulse had regulated. After taking a quick swig from the beer bottle he smuggled under his coat, he drew me close with his arm. "You okay, Kel?"

I nodded with my eyes closed. "Just a little too much for me in there."

He pulled me toward him, half whispering and half slurring, "I'm sorry, Kel, I swear I'll shape up. I'll make this year the best year of your life. I love you."

"I love you, too."

Wayne brushed a snowflake off my eyelash then cupped my chin and sultrily murmured, "Happy New

Year," with the boisterous countdown echoing from inside. At the stroke of midnight, my quivering lips reluctantly melted under his fiery kiss.

****

"Hey, you. Happy New Year." Shannon sprang into my classroom on the morning of our first day back to school.

"Happy, happy." A smile dangled on the corner of her mouth, and I stopped placing my first period's bellwork on the desks. "Okay, what's going on?"

"Sorry I didn't call you back." She slyly winked. "I was, well, busy."

"Busy, you say?" I raised my eyebrow. "Busy doing what?"

"Oh, I don't know." Shannon casually replied while impishly curling a strand of her ginger hair around her finger, then she hopped a few times in place as her grin grew larger. "Lots to tell you. I have to work through lunch and planning period today to catch up on what I blew off during break, but lots to tell. How was your week off?"

"Better than I expected, including *Portrait*."

"That's my girl. I'll swing by after school to gab." She shot out of the room and across the hall like a firecracker.

The first school day of the new calendar year lumbered by at a snail's pace, particularly since I ate lunch alone and spent my planning period grading instead of kibitzing with Shannon. When the last bell sounded, I bid farewell to my boisterous students then sketched out lesson ideas while shifting my gaze from my wristwatch to the classroom clock to make sure the times matched up.

Shannon eventually burst into the room and joyously greeted me with her trademark, "Hey, you."

I perceived a faint yodel in the hallway so I suggested, "Let's sneak out of here and head over to The Gutter. I'd rather be by ourselves to catch up, plus I could go for a caffeine pick-me-up right about now."

"Marvelous idea. Meet you there in ten."

She snuck across the hall while I assembled what I needed to bring home into my satchel. I quietly crept out of my classroom, tiptoed down the hall, and reached my car without Monica's verbose talons ensnaring me.

The Gutter's amiable climate and my signature latte were the perfect prescription for comfort and just what I needed. I cozied in my favorite chair, the plush sky blue one with the matching footrest alongside the back window and away from the hubbub of the tables. I journaled as I waited for Shannon, who surfaced out of nowhere with a chai tea.

"Sorry I'm late." She crossed her eyes as she hung her black peacoat on the nearest hook, then lowered herself into the purple rocker next to me. "I stumbled upon Monica on my way out and she bent my ear for longer than I hoped. Just what we were trying to avoid."

"Okay, I've been dying all day." I set aside my notebook and implored, "Tell me what's behind the silly, giddy grin you've got going on."

"I will, but parts of what I'm about to tell you I cannot believe, it so mysteriously landed in my lap."

"What? What landed in your lap?"

Shannon nonchalantly sipped her chai wearing a wily smirk until I couldn't stand it anymore. "Spill the beans," I bellowed and jokingly kicked her foot with mine.

"Here's the scoop. Oliver traveled up to Boston the day after Christmas for business meetings, so I tagged along and we made the trip into a short getaway. We got home late last night, and boy, I am bushed."

"You don't seem tired at all. You look…" I gave her the once over from head to toe. "Overjoyed. Yes, absolutely overjoyed."

"I am, and I feel something I haven't felt in, like, forever but it's hard for me to explain it."

"Because of Boston?"

"Because of something that happened in Boston."

"You're simply beaming, so whatever happened has to be good."

"I love Oliver now more than ever." She gazed dreamily at the wall in front of us. "My heart, it always pined for that someone special I knew was out there waiting for me, and I knew early on in our relationship that it wasn't Dan. I stayed with him for much too long out of obligation, not because I loved him. Well, I found that person, and it's Oliver. He cares about me, he supports me, and we fit perfectly together like puzzle pieces. But, there's more…"

Shannon lobbed a brochure onto my lap.

"What's this?" I picked the flyer up and read its title aloud. " 'Boston College International Program in Dublin, Ireland?' " I cried out, "Oh, Shan, this is magnificent."

"I know." She jumped to her feet, overcome with excitement. "I heard about this program years ago, but I always figured I was too old or it was too late. While Oliver was in his meetings, I went out for a drive and found myself meeting with a graduate school admissions counselor on the campus of Boston College. The program is perfect, everything I could ever want, and it's completely possible for me to do."

"Really? You can teach here while being enrolled in the Boston program at the same time?"

"Believe it or not, I can." She nodded with vigor and sat back down. "I'm already registered to take three classes on campus this summer. Next school year, I'll take two distance-learning classes during both the fall and spring semesters, then I'll leave for Ireland after Watertown's graduation and be an official post-grad student in their Dublin affiliate's summer program." She raised her arms in a V shape. "I have a purpose now, earning my Masters of Arts in Irish Literature and Culture, and the opportunity to both learn and live in Dublin is my dream come true."

I exploded from my chair and hugged her tight. "I'm so happy for you. Oliver, will he go with you when you are studying in Boston or Dublin?"

"No, he told me I needed to do this for myself. Being apart during the next two summers will be difficult, and there's no doubt I'm setting myself up for a crap ton of work, but everything will be sooooo worth it." She kept a count on her right hand. "I'll visit the Martello Tower and Sweny's from *Ulysses*, shop along Grafton, and, no doubt, down many a pint in many a pub."

"Fantastic."

She flashed her eyes to the left and to the right and then leaned in close. "You know, something has always been missing. More than Oliver and more than my job as a teacher. Something is just missing from here." She patted the center of her chest. "But I am confident pursuing this degree and learning in Dublin will fill my soul's hole, like you fill yours with writing."

"I'm delighted for you, Shan. And guess what?"

"What?"

"I am writing again, not just journaling, but writing for real. I guess the same universe which led you to your Dublin destiny was working double time by sending words my way."

"See?" Shannon giggled with glee. "And I bet Joyce inspired your fingers to write with a pen or type on your keyboard again, right?"

"Maybe. When I read your inscription, I wondered, how can you always see the writer in my soul, since I abandoned her so long ago?"

"Gut instinct," she answered with unwavering certainty. "From the moment we met, I felt a natural and deep connection with you. Your art is writing, and like Stephen Dedalus, you're a person who has already undergone many transformations. But there's more to come, and your art will show you the way. On the flip side, like Joyce, your writing will be a service to your community."

"You're the only one who can see the real me underneath all of this." I circled my finger in the air in front of my forehead. "Tell me, though. Why Joyce?"

"Hold that thought." Shannon ordered an iced tea for herself and two of The Gutter's signature double-chocolate loaded brownies.

I wrote, "transformation, art, words, craft, service" in my notebook, then Shannon handed me one of the brownies, which weighed at least half a pound.

"Why Joyce, you ask? For starters, I am 100 percent Irish. Secondly, many find his stream-of-consciousness style awkward, but I find it natural to understand that kind of writing. Not many people read *Ulysses* for fun, but I have, several times now. Joyce is the stream-of-consciousness master, for sure, but underneath his pretentiousness, Joyce perceives the value in the average, and since I am average, I can relate."

"Let me tell you something, Shannon. You are way more than average. I admit I enjoyed *Portrait* more than I thought I would, and 'Araby' wasn't too bad, either. But reading *Ulysses* for fun?" I scrunched up my nose before taking a gigantic bite out of my brownie.

"I'll let you cruise through the rest of the school year because you'll be busy enough with teaching, grading, and writing, but you better buck up, camper, because *Ulysses* is on your summer reading list."

"No"—I pouted in jest—"please, teacher, don't make me."

"Now, now, you've got to reap the harvest of Joyce's wisdom and savor his example. The writer in you will be glad you did."

"The truth is, I doubt myself as a writer."

"Why?"

I turned my head away. "It's a long story."

"Listen, I just confessed some deep shit to you, so lay it on me, Kel."

"Okay—" I took a deep breath. "—here goes. I loved to write when I was little and wanted to be a writer when I grew up. I escaped my mother's control by writing story after story and coped with my situation by putting my feelings on paper instead of letting them build up in my mind. I buried every page I scribbled on, every notebook, in the toy box inside my closet. Every night, I'd pray she would never find them, because if she read just one…"

"Let me guess. She found them, right?"

"Of course she did." I scowled. "On the day before I left for college, I entered my room to carry another packed tote to the car and found the toy box open and her reading from one of my notebooks."

"Oh. boy."

"She screamed at me, accused me of lying about her in what I wrote, called me an ungrateful bitch who was lucky to have such a caring mother. I stood there, dumbfounded, then out of nowhere, she slugged me square in my face. Blood flowed from my nose like a fountain. I grabbed a shirt off the floor and held it to my nose while she lugged the toy box out of my closet and heaved it down the staircase. I burst into tears the moment the box cracked against the tile landing at the bottom and fractured into a gazillion fragments. Instead of consoling me, she grabbed my arm and dragged me down the stairs behind her."

Shannon covered her mouth with her hand and whispered, "How horrible."

"She forced me to stand next to her as she pitched each notebook and piece of paper into the fireplace while raging about how I should have never been born. I could taste the bile rising from my stomach. The last notebook, she held it out toward me, flicked a lighter, and lit the corner before lobbing it on top of the pile. As they caught fire and burned, her face cracked into a sick kind of vindictive pleasure, almost demonic. Those flames extinguished my desire to write and destroyed my dreams of being a writer."

"Jesus, Kel, I had no idea, but now I understand. No child should have to endure such abusive lunacy. I'm sorry if I caused you any discomfort by urging you to write."

"Actually, you helped me come to terms with the words still burning inside me, regardless of how much I try to deny them." I nodded. "Freeing them is going to take some time, but writing is a comfort again, and dare I say, might be my passion, like Dublin is yours. But another problem is I've never seen most of the places I want to use as settings for my stories. How can I write when I've been nowhere and done nothing worth writing about?"

"Once again, it all circles back to Joyce. Sure, he lived in Dublin, Paris, and Zurich, but he used Dublin as the setting for most of his pieces. You don't have an anchor tethered to your ankles, and you don't have to be stuck here in Watertown forever. Write what you know, and the rest will take care of itself. Get out there, see the world, and live, dammit. Let me ask, have things on the home front improved at all?"

"A little. We spent a good amount of time together over the break. Enjoyable time, too."

"Oliver is my soulmate, and every day, our relationship is better than its yesterday. I hope your relationship with Wayne continues to improve." Shannon gazed at the moving eyes and tail of the vintage black-and-white cat clock hanging on the wall opposite us and she vaulted out of her chair. "Crap, I'm supposed to meet Oliver and I'm going to be late. See you tomorrow morning." Shannon dashed out of The Gutter in a frenzy with her crimson scarf trailing behind her.

I envied Shannon's serendipity in encountering both her soulmate and her life's purpose.

She deserved to be happy.

But then again, so did I.

****

Although my marriage appeared to have improved at the cusp of the new year, its mask soon fell off and Wayne again reverted to spending more time at The Rip Tide than at home.

And I really didn't care.

Fate handed me another incentive to shut my eyes to my deteriorating home life when Del went under the knife for unexpected knee surgery in mid March. I undertook teaching one of her classes and advising the spirit booster club in her absence for the remainder of the school year. I lost my planning period but gained an opportunity to branch out in new directions and, with any luck, make a difference in the lives of more students.

Shannon and I still dropped in at Delancy's on Friday afternoons to socialize, but neither of us stayed for more than an hour or so. We'd meander and mingle, discuss life for a while at the backside of the bar, then slip out of the side door before having to witness anything unsavory that might result from the free-flowing pints and cocktails.

Spring's end-of-the-school-year traditions rapidly breezed in, every day more of a whirlwind than the last. My biggest accomplishment as a first-year educator was my students' measurable improvement in their writing from when we first met back in September, evidenced by their standardized test scores. I selected five essays for a state high school writing contest. Martin's work won second place and the other four earned honorable mentions. The board of education renewed my teaching contract and recognized Martin for his state writing award at their May meeting.

I cleansed the distaste from my own disastrous experience and chaperoned the prom, which had the distinction of being the first event ever held at The Ardmore, a brand new elegant banquet facility just up from Delancy's on the Boulevard. The evening was just lovely. I took pictures with my students who were there and hung a collage I made from the photographs in my classroom.

My department chose me to present the English students-of-the-year certificates at Waterville's annual academic awards night, and I helped distribute diplomas after taking part in the graduation processional held the night before the last day of school.

After the graduates received their diplomas and said their final farewells, I headed out into the twilight with Shannon. "Don't look now, but this is your summer reading assignment." She smirked and slipped a book into my bag.

I snuck a peek then stomped my foot like a toddler having a temper tantrum and whined, "Oh, no, *Ulysses*?"

"It is time. You've kept an open mind about James Joyce up to this point, and you said in your own words *Portrait* wasn't terrible. Have I ever steered you wrong? Just trust me and read it. And consider living a little more outside of your comfort zone. A life of adventure leads to wonderful stories to be told." She hugged me and encouraged, "Believe me, you're bigger than this, my friend."

I squeezed her back but wholeheartedly disagreed. I wasn't bigger than anything.

****

The last day of school at Waterville High School was an abbreviated schedule with just underclass students required to attend classes. At dismissal, the entire Waterville staff convened in front of the school to wave farewell as the busses, filled with students cheering and flailing their arms out the windows, pulled away for the last time until September. When the last one hooked a left from Davis Drive onto the Boulevard, Al triggered a confetti canister and everyone applauded, except for the custodians who were relegated to clean up the mess.

"So, where are we going to celebrate the end of the year?" Rob Fields yelled.

"Dominick's Deck," the physical education teachers said.

"Delancy's," Monica yodeled.

Al chimed in, "The Rip Tide."

Rob tallied the votes, and cheers erupted as he declared Dominick's Deck the winner.

"I used to work there," I said to Shannon. "Are you going?"

"I wouldn't miss it. Everybody goes to the last-day-of-school shindig, even lunch lady Olga."

I giggled. "No way."

"I'm 100 percent serious. You'll see. I'll meet you there."

Seven years had passed since I last strode the boardwalk to the tiki deck half a mile south of and parallel with Smuggler's. Chills rushed over my skin like spilled ice water as I set my eyes on the sign for the landmark Dominick's Deck, and I shuddered at recalling the devastating defeat that shrouded me during the post 0.0 summer. The Deck became my safe haven back then, and I clocked in as many hours as possible between Memorial Day and Labor Day while forking over all of my earnings to my mother in a paltry attempt to pay off my squandered semester.

I thought about how much I endured since then and

the small victories along my way, shook off the shivers, and lifted my head high.

I hadn't seen Dominic Scotto, the namesake of Dominick's Deck since my last day at the end of that season, but I'd be able to pick him out of a lineup for the rest of my life. While an apprentice chef right out of high school, he created the culinary masterpiece known up and down the eastern seaboard as "Dom's Famous Fries"—fresh-cut Idaho potatoes deep fried in peanut oil then hand tossed with sea salt, vinegar, and a secret seasoning blend. His fries were featured on several nationwide culinary cable shows, with one crowning him with the coveted title of "America's Fries Prize."

I slowed my pace entering the tiki deck and spied Dom taking pride in the business he built from the ground up by wiping down tables himself. He must have sensed someone lurking behind him because he stalled in mid-wipe motion and slowly angled his head in my direction. His puzzled eyes lit up when they connected with mine.

"Kelly, my dear, how are you?" He cackled and threw his solid, husky arms around me.

"Good, Dom. Glad to see you're still as jovial as ever."

"I have to be. Otherwise, I'd run away from the self-centered tourists who frequent this place. You always handled them with graciousness, and you never complained." Dom whispered into my ear, "You were one of a kind, Miss Kelly. One of a kind." My colleagues showed up in spurts and he inquired, "So, these people waving to you, they aren't vacationers, are they?"

"They sure are. I led them single file all the way from the Garden State Parkway so you can take them for all they're worth."

He frowned at me and crossed his arms in mock disapproval. "You still have the worst poker face of all time, young lady."

I giggled. "Actually, they are my fellow teachers and coworkers at Waterville High School."

"A teacher? I thought you worked for that newfangled computer place."

"I did, but I took classes at night to finish my degree and I started teaching in September."

"Wonderful." Dom cheered and pulled me into another bear hug. He then boomed to the staff, "Anything this young lady orders today is on the house. Understand? Anything."

My cheeks warmed again. "You don't have to do that, Dom."

"Your money is no good here." Then he bellowed, "And half off anything ordered by Kelly's coworkers, too, including the bar." Applause rose from the Stingray staff assembled down on the deck with Del leading a "Go Kelly" cheer from her wheelchair.

"Thanks again, Dom."

"You bet. Please, don't be a stranger."

"Will do." I gave him a peck on his forehead and headed over to where Del was still whooping. "Del, what a surprise. I wasn't aware you would be here."

"I felt so great, I thought going for a jog on the beach would be a fabulous idea. Ended up tearing my ACL, so I'm scheduled for another surgery next week. There goes my summer, but half off drinks makes things a little better, chickee."

I ordered my usual seltzer with lemon and filled Del in about the students she had until she went out on medical leave. When I told her Lou Austin passed for the year, she raised her eyebrow. "I can't believe it. Did you help him, or did he legit pass?"

"He legit passed. Completed his assignments on time and even presented one of the best final projects about *The Outsiders*."

"He did absolutely nothing for me. Nice job, Kel. Hey, it just registered…we're Del and Kel." Del shouted down the bar, "Hey, Mon. Look, we're Del and Kel."

Monica good humoredly yodeled, "Kel, I won't let you steal my Del."

A "Del and Kel" rhyme session followed with everyone vying for the best verse. Al prowled up from behind and his ridicule made the hairs on my neck stand at attention. "Del and Kel can go to hell."

I cocked my head and replied, "Maybe I'll tell Dom to charge you double for everything you order. Would you like that, instead?"

My unexpected comeback took the words right out of his mouth. As he slithered away, a rush of gratifying fulfilment at standing up for myself overcame me, and I kind of liked it.

Donning her trademark tortoise-shell sunglasses, Shannon scampered over and jubilantly saluted. "Hey, you. Happy summer, indeed." She raised her pint of beer to my seltzer and we clinked glasses.

"You can't toast without us," Monica squealed and brought her daiquiri level with Del's and we clinked again.

Al and Dan were deep in conversation on the other side of the bar, and all of a sudden, their eyes narrowed and they shifted their heads toward us in unison. I warned, "Heads up," under my breath to Shannon.

"What?"

"Right before you got here, Al was being his usual, weaselly self, and now he's staring us down. Dan too."

Shannon seethed while kicking her foot on the bottom rung of my stool, the low, metallic clonking sound increasing in both rhythm and volume. She shot lasers at them and growled, "Those sons of bitches." She hopped off her barstool and marched over to them, but I couldn't hear what she said. Al stormed out, and Dan idled over to where Phil Nice was sweettalking Olga the lunch lady into doing a shot.

Shannon reappeared at my side, released her clenched fists, and chugged her beer. "Infuriating. Those assclowns had that coming."

"I will forever be in awe of your ability to make a scene without making a scene. You're the ninja of conflict."

"Indeed I am, my friend. I can't believe I leave for Boston in two days."

"You are going to have the most amazing time. After you get back, let's get together." I sipped my seltzer and spotted an obvious tourist with dark hair and dark eyebrows spilling over his outdated, amber-lensed sunglasses ordering a drink near Olga and her menagerie.

"Check out that imbecile." I pointed and laughed at the newcomer. "When will these freaking vacationers learn wearing hideous tropical shirts and dark socks with sandals is like wearing a placard with the words 'I'm not a local' written on it?"

"He's here," Shannon squealed with pleasure and whisked over to the man in the tacky clothing. Oliver locked her in an embrace, then he handed her a beer and they headed in my direction.

Enduring the Waves

I hung my head in disgrace and stammered, "I'm...I'm so sorry. I should learn to keep my mouth shut."

"Kel, you're a riot, and really, it's no big deal." Shannon laughed. "Please allow me to formally introduce you to Oliver O'Shea, the archetypal mismatched tourist and the absolute love of my life."

"Pleased to meet you, Kelly." Oliver smiled and extended his hand to me in spite of my blunder. "Shannon's told me a lot about you."

"Likewise, Oliver." I returned his handshake with my face as red as Dominick's lobster claw special. "Happy to meet you."

We drifted over to where the Waterville staff along with a group of random bar patrons chanted Olga's name, and everyone hooted and hollered after she threw back her first shot ever. Just then, the legendary opening riff of a song advising listeners to never stop believing blasted through the speakers and overpowered the bar noise. A memory featuring the same song flitted through my mind and a disconcerting ache dripping with nostalgia trickled through my veins...

On the night of my first date with Wayne, we parked at Smuggler's after dinner. The lead singer's unmistakable tenor-alto voice filled the car as Wayne told me about the girl of his dreams on the jetty who was writing while surrounded by the moon. "It sure was tough to keep believing at times, but he's right, because here you are," Wayne murmured and kissed me like I had never been kissed before. A multitude of butterflies released into my stomach under the waning moon and the shimmering stars...

I shook with a shock. Once I reacclimated to the

present, my gaze fell upon Dan. He glowered at Shannon and Oliver from the other side of the bar, her head resting on Oliver's chest and wearing a contented smile while swaying in time to the music. When Dan realized I saw him, he punched his fists into the pockets of his shorts and charged out of the Deck.

"Kelllll-eeeeee," Monica yodeled, "order us a few apps so they're free. Dom's Fries and mozz sticks and Bahama dogs."

"You got it, Mon."

I placed the order then stepped back along the sidelines to observe the scene surrounding me. Del wheeled in time to the syncopated beat resounding through the floor, and when the music segued to a tropical high-rhythm number featuring steel drums, she snatched a broom from the busboy and commanded a limbo be started toot sweet.

My colleagues laughed and limboed under the stick one after another, but something just didn't sit right with me. For a reason I couldn't identify, I felt like an outsider more than I ever had with my Waterville family.

With clammy hands and my insides feeling as if I was plummeting from a cliff, I slipped out, unnoticed, and headed home without saying goodbye to anyone.

****

Ahhh, summer.

My favorite season.

I savored the opportunity to relax and take each summer day as it came, which included using the bathroom whenever nature called and eating when I was hungry, not because a bell announced my lunch time. I renewed my vow of writing every day at Smuggler's, and the idea of spending my days at the real inlet instead of gawking at the replica spanning a wall thrilled me.

However, my first trip there on day one of summer break did not pan out as I hoped.

I skipped a step or two in the parking lot after snagging the last available spot and scaled the rocks with care to my former go-to writing site. I fanned my blanket in the breeze and allowed it to float down upon the flat rock, and after I lowered myself on it, I fired up my laptop with a few angle corrections so I could view the screen through the blinding sun. After a generous swig of water, I examined my surroundings with my fingers perched on my keyboard and waited for something in the scenery to spark my words.

And…nothing.

I studied the waves, then the boats fighting the incoming tide.

Nothing.

I observed the diving cormorant through the rainbow created by the current's spray.

Nothing.

I scratched at my cuticles and stared more than I typed, my eyes hastily shifting from my keyboard to my surroundings in a futile effort to coax out the elusive words. I thought my new mindset would be the catalyst for my words to flow, but I was wrong.

Dead wrong.

I sat there stewing. Out of the blue, an unnerving apprehension consumed me. I had never run into my parents since leaving home, but prickles scattered over my skin. I nervously peered over my shoulder at every car I heard behind me, expecting to see my mother at the wheel.

The dread soon unbearable, I trudged to my car and

betrayed my hometown by migrating to Glenharbor. Even though a bird could fly across the waterway in mere seconds, it took me forever and a day to get to that side of the inlet. I backtracked to the main strip, sat in traffic at the drawbridge which opened for a sailboat, and waited near Glenharbor Station for the noon train to pick up its passengers. Once the gates rose, I searched for an unoccupied parking spot up by the beach, which on a summer afternoon at the shore could be as difficult as finding a grain of rice in the sand. It took me three loops through the lot until I found someone who appeared to be leaving. I tailed her and waited with my blinker on for her to back out of the coveted parking spot, then almost got into a screaming match with a tourist who sought to steal it from me.

Agitated and disturbed, I schlepped to the jetty and plopped down across from where I set up shop earlier. "Okay, I've got my laptop. I've got the passing vessels, the ocean and the foghorn, everything I need for inspiration," I loudly declared. A fisherman on the rocks below me jerked his head in my direction. "Sorry, buddy," I yelled. "Just talking to myself." He grimaced and re-hooked his line with a fresh clam then cast it into the outgoing tide.

The ocean's wind stroking my left cheek in contrast to my usual right made me uneasy, the reversed vantage proved fruitless in jarring writing fluency. I mindlessly transitioned into a part of the landscape, an insignificant detail in a massive masterpiece, while my words remained suffocated.

At noon, I counted six party boats returning from a morning of bottom fishing and heading toward their respective docks. A short time later, they paraded back through the inlet in a long procession embarking on their afternoon fishing excursions, their rails filled with new patrons gripping their rods and nets. The boats sliced through the screaming current where the inlet met the sea and fanned off into their captain's chosen direction, each hoping his secret honey hole would yield the most fish.

My honey hole of words for the day, however, would yield no bounty.

"This is bullshit," I griped under my breath.

I crammed my laptop and my water bottle into my backpack and trekked over to the surfing beach. With its combination of sandbars, swells, and currents creating a one-of-a-kind break along the north wall of the jetty, some of the world's best surfers have been known to frequent Glenharbor's legendary break line.

Today's lack of wind and resulting glassy conditions chased them away, the waves as barren as my screen.

With no surfers to entertain me, I strolled along Glenharbor's asphalt walkway spanning from the jetty to the north end of town and about five hundred yards inland from the ocean. The blacktop footpath was notorious for burning the bottoms of many unsuspecting bare feet on sweltering summer days.

I came to a standstill when I spotted a royal blue sticker from Stubby's Surf Shop on a "No Dogs Allowed" sign. It was a rite of passage for locals like me who grew up at the shore to deface street signs by slapping stickers from local surf shops, bands, and eateries onto them. Yes, putting stickers on town-owned signs was technically vandalism, but most police officers looked the other way because they were just as guilty of defacing the signs with stickers in their youth. Stubby's was down the street from my childhood home, and I always had a pocketful of their stickers ready to slam on signs while peddling around town. Another influx of wistful discomfort surged through my core at seeing their distinctive logo with the longboard inside the turquoise waves.

As pressure from a quick-moving weather front built in the air, a wall of clouds concealed the sun without warning so I headed back to my car and arrived home a writing disappointment. I fixed myself a plate of grapes, cheese, and crackers and wasted more time stewing than eating.

"What am I doing?" I grumbled aloud. "A whole lot of nothing, that's what I'm doing."

I covered my dish with plastic wrap, put it into the refrigerator, and lumbered to the Smuggler's room, where I gawked at the fake inlet the same way I gaped at the real one earlier.

Nothing came, no words or ideas or thoughts, but I refused to end the day with zero to show for it. I forced myself to scrawl a terrible paragraph in haste about the stickered signs, then slammed my laptop shut.

A beam of the early evening's sunlight broke through the waning storm clouds to stream through the window and illuminate the copy of *Ulysses* sitting next to me. A revelation I must have filed away from a conversation with Shannon came to the forefront of my mind—the entire volume of *Ulysses* took place on one day, June 16, 1904.

I confirmed the day's date in my planner—June 16.

Well played, universe. Well played.

I curled up and turned to the first chapter titled "Telemachus," and at once remembered the character Stephen Dedalus from *Portrait*. About ten pages in, with my eyelids weighty, I drifted off to sleep alongside visions of Stephen singing loud along the Smuggler's Inlet wall and the fishermen frowning at him in contempt.

****

Days two and three of my summer were the same—a great deal of gawping at both the real and fake Smuggler's without writing much of anything. After a valiant effort to read "Telemachus," I felt like a simpleton because I couldn't quite grasp everything on my own. I didn't want to bother Shannon since she was busy with her studies in Boston, so I borrowed two literary analysis books from the Waterville Public Library. I planned to read a chapter of *Ulysses* while taking my own notes, then delve into the analysis books to help me comprehend what I read before moving on to the next chapter.

At three in the morning of summer's day four, I jolted awake dripping with sweat. Disoriented, I caught my breath and stumbled to the kitchen, guzzled a full glass of water, and wiped my forehead with a wet paper towel.

I planted my right cheek on the cool granite countertop and couldn't for the life of me remember what I had dreamt about, but whatever it was, it shocked me something fierce.

"Kel? You okay?" Wayne groggily mumbled after wandering in. It was the first time I had seen him in days.

"I must have had a bad dream or something. Sorry I woke you."

"Fell asleep on the couch." He grabbed a bottle from the refrigerator, took a giant drink from it, then gagged and spit into the sink. "Dammit, what is this, ketchup?"

He heaved the bottle into the trash basket and grabbed another from the refrigerator's bottom shelf. After making sure it was water, he asked, "You gonna be okay?"

I nodded with the side of my face still smushed on the countertop. "Yeah, I'll be fine."

"Love ya." He tousled my hair and headed to the bedroom.

Instead of answering him back, I shifted down the counter and switched cheeks for a few minutes then dragged myself back to the Smuggler's room. I readjusted my head on my pillow and snuggled the top edge of my blanket under my chin, but I couldn't fall asleep. I counted sheep, then fishing boats sailing out of the inlet, then classroom desks, but my mind didn't power down.

Rather, it accelerated.

The running soundtrack of possible "what ifs" literally about nothing sounded its dissonance in my brain and made it impossible to relax while that damn hamster running at top speed inside my mind's wheel refused to slow down. The delirious visions persisted, the unending fancies twisted into terrors until I couldn't take it anymore.

I tossed off the covers, grasped my pen and held its tip to my notebook's page, but nothing came.

What the hell was wrong with me?

I powered up my laptop, but the inability to type anything coherent only confounded my frustration. My mind just spun too many fascinatingly disturbing imaginations to count, but when I sought to write about them, it turned as white as the sneering screen in front of me.

I whimpered and typed, "Maybe this is what I need, maybe I am meant to be a blubbering idiot over nothing."

The floodgates then opened and tears streamed down my face. I curled up in the fetal position and allowed the uncontrollable convulsions to have their way with me, but I muffled my cries because I didn't want Wayne to hear me in the other room.

It took me about an hour to regroup after my ridiculous meltdown and would have headed up to the beach for the sunrise if it wasn't drizzling outside. I mindlessly checked my email, and the first message in my inbox provided me with a purpose—the student leadership program at the high school was hosting a blood drive later that morning.

Even though I never donated blood before, making a difference in someone else's life was preferable to wallowing in my pathetic existential crisis.

After showering and drinking two bottles of water, I set off for the school's gymnasium and was the second person in line. I filled out the required application, and when I came to the box for my blood type, I hesitated.

My blood type?

I faintly recollected my father once making a big deal about how he had the best blood because almost anyone could use type O, which he claimed stood for outstanding. My mother refused to be bested and condescendingly refuted her "Grade A" blood was, in fact, superior to both his and my type O outstanding value.

Asshats.

I checked the box for O, signed and dated the form, and handed it to one of the student volunteers, who directed me to Cot Two. A nurse greeted me, "Hello, my name is Kathy. We're grateful you're here today. There's a critical blood shortage at the Jersey Shore right now and every donation helps. I'll have you hooked up in no time. Extend your index finger so I can perform a rapid test to confirm your blood type."

"I filled it out on my form, it's O." I sat upright on the cot and stuck out my right index finger.

Nurse Kathy pricked my fingertip in a flash then applied a strip to the globe of blood that formed and handed me a cotton ball. "Apply pressure with the cotton to your finger to stop the bleeding." She talked as she transferred my blood onto a card filled with rows of circles. "You'd be surprised how many people are wrong about their blood type. We have to accurately label the sample from every donor so it doesn't go to someone by mistake and kill 'em. Now, lie back and we'll get started."

I did as Nurse Kathy instructed, and she suddenly made a clicking sound with her tongue. "See? It's a good thing we checked. Your blood type is AB."

I shook my head. "That's impossible. My mother has type A and my father has O."

She connected plastic tubes and apparatus to my arm while she explained, "Our test is 100 percent accurate. Perhaps you were mistaken about your father, I mean, his blood type. The donation process takes roughly fifteen minutes. After a snack and a little rest, you'll be on your way. Your donation in particular is valuable because with AB blood, you are a universal plasma donor."

Mistaken about my father? Why would she have said such a thing?

I remained as still as I could, but thoughts raced

inside my head.

How could I have been wrong about my blood type? I was certain my father had blood type O. Could it be that...

"Are you all right, dear? Your pulse is rising and you're as white as a sheet. It's okay"—Nurse Kathy rubbed my arm—"try to relax..."

She then yelled, "Can someone give me a hand here?" Her words echoed in my mind like they were bouncing on metal, then the fluorescent lights suspended from the ceiling rapidly tunneled away from me and I succumbed to the darkness.

****

I blinked my eyes open to three unfamiliar and blurry faces surrounded by the brightest of lights staring down at me from above.

I assumed I was in heaven and the faces were angels ready to sing my name in glory, but they shouted it, instead. After inhaling an absolutely revolting odor, I lurched forward and things gradually came into focus: the bleachers, the basketball nets hanging from the ceiling, the silver Stingray painted on the black wall.

Criminy.

I wasn't floating outside of the pearly gates.

I was in Waterville's gymnasium.

As I regained consciousness, concern for me faded, and the other blood drive staffers dispersed. Nurse Kathy prevented me when I stood up. "Not yet, Kelly. You'll have to wait here a while."

I shook my head. "But..."

"No buts. Drink some water and eat these graham crackers. Relax and you'll be able to leave soon."

I had no choice but to acquiesce. My tongue grew

less furry with every swallow of water, and I chewed the cardboard-like squares covered with too much cinnamon and not enough sugar while staring intently at the clock on the wall. Exasperation built behind my forehead with every spring forward of the second hand, which advanced slower than a tortoise. After a little over an hour, Nurse Kathy and the medical chief both agreed I was cleared to leave.

I drove home confounded and dropped onto the couch just as Wayne emerged from the kitchen with a pork roll, egg, and cheese sandwich.

"Want one?" he offered, then he set down his breakfast after hearing my whimpers. "What's wrong, Kel? What happened?"

I wiped my eyes with my trembling palms. "I wanted to donate blood at the high school this morning, and I told them my blood type was O."

"And?"

"They tested my blood. The results were type AB."

"So?"

"My mother's blood type is A, and my father's is type O. I know that for a fact." My mouth twisted. "It can only mean one thing…"

Wayne ceased rubbing my back and exclaimed, "Really?"

I resumed bawling and cried out, "Yes, Wayne. Really." I fought to say it. "It's got…it's got…to be that, right? It's got to be…my father…my father isn't…"

"Maybe you should call Christian, see if he knows anything about this."

"What do I even say to him? 'Hey, Christian, do you know if we have the same father or if I'm the bastard of the family?' " I flailed my arms then plunged backward while my pulse soared as my world imploded and reduced to rubble. I focused on the white ceiling for a few minutes, then I yelled, "What's the difference, dammit!"

I grabbed the phone and dialed Christian's number.

He answered after two rings. "Hey, sis. It's early. Everything okay?"

"I'm not sure, Christian."

"What's wrong? What's going on?"

I took a deep breath and asked, "Do you know your blood type?"

"Yes, I'm O. Diego and I have our blood tested every six months for, well, you know."

"I thought I had O too. Dad has O and Mom has A."

"You are correct about Dad and Mom."

"But I'm not O or A."

"Come again?"

"They tested my blood before I donated at a blood drive this morning. One hundred percent certain my blood type is AB."

Christian hesitated then blurted out, "But…but that makes no sense."

"It makes sense, if it's what I think it is."

"No, it can't be."

"It's the only possible explanation, Christian."

We were both quiet for a spell, then his voice echoed in the abyss, "Holy shit, Kel. This is unreal."

"What am I going to do?" I wailed.

"I guess, first, figure out if pursuing the truth really matters. If your hunch is correct, maybe it's the reason why they were so deplorable to you. Not that I'm excusing their behavior by any means, but it sure would explain a hell of a lot. Would you be comfortable going over to Dad's and point blank asking him, without a confrontation or anything, just ask him to explain it?"

"I never thought I'd see either of them again, but I'd definitely rather deal with him than her."

"If it were me, I'd want to know."

"Damn," I croaked. "This is real."

"You're stronger than anyone I've ever met, Kel, but all your life, you ran away from this and that and the other. Don't run away from this. You deserve to know who you are."

"I...but I've never really known who I am."

"I'll tell you who you are. You are my sister, no matter what, and I love you."

"I love you, too."

I hung up and lowered my head into my hands. Wayne brought me a cup of tea and a toasted blueberry muffin. "I used the Kerrygold butter you love so much. You've got to eat something, Kel."

"I know."

"You're a big girl, but I'm here for you if you need me. Always."

I ate the muffin and drank the tea in silence while Wayne showered. I considered every possible scenario for learning the truth, and all of them had one thing in common—I had to do it in person.

"So, what are you going to do?" Wayne walked in, freshly dressed and drying his wet hair with a towel.

"My father, geez, can I still refer to him as my father? He used to get home from work around four. I guess I'll play detective and plan my own stakeout. Then when I see him? I just don't know..."

"You don't have to deal with this today if you're not ready."

"Yes, I do—" I nodded. "—like Christian said, I've been escaping my whole life. It's time to quit running away and pull up my big-girl pants. I need to face this head on and get answers."

Wayne kissed my hand then gazed into my eyes in a vain endeavor to eliminate my distress through the magic of his blues.

It didn't work.

I changed into my long turquoise sundress and my multi-colored sandals, the same outfit I wore for Waterville High School's awards night in May.

The day was a scorcher, brimming with excruciating humidity formed by the morning rain's hangover, so I pulled my hair up but left a few wisps hanging loosely here and there. I dropped my triskele into my dress pocket and saw it was already three in the afternoon. Wayne once again offered to go with me but I declined. "Could you do me a favor and stay here tonight instead of going to The Rip Tide? Please. I need you."

"I'll be here when you get back," he assured me.

Christian was right. It was time to stop running.

I embarked upon my journey of truth and drove in a surreal fog past Stubby's Surf Shop for the first time in eons then turned right onto Seacrest Court.

I parked down the street from my childhood home under a massive maple tree but kept the engine running so the air conditioning would keep me cool. I was confident my father wouldn't recognize my silver sedan because I owned a beat-up green hatchback when I left home.

His pickup truck's sputtering engine ground in my ears before I even saw it and made my heart thump harder. I couldn't believe that hunk of junk was still running. He blindly passed by me in his black rust bucket, and as he turned left into the driveway, I killed my ignition.

I told myself I could do this then exited my car, my sunglasses fogging up almost immediately from the humidity. I removed them and dried the lenses with my dress, then put them back on. He was already on the porch with his key in the doorknob by the time I arrived at the bottom of the driveway.

I called, "Hello?"

He whipped his head around, squinted, and then stammered, "Kel, Kel, Kelly?"

"Yeah, it's me." I kept up a cool exterior while paying no heed to my sweaty palms or my ready-to-buckle knees.

He stood with his mouth open for a bit, then remarked, "You're so grown up. How have you been?"

"Pretty good. I'm married and I finished college last year. I'm a teacher now."

"Wow, a teacher—" His weathered face softened. "—at what school?"

"Waterville High School. I teach English."

"You were always reading and writing."

We stood in awkward silence before I mustered up the courage to spark the conversation we had to have. "Listen, do you have a minute so we could talk, maybe sit here on the porch for a few?"

"If it's money you need, I have none to give you," he snapped. "Your mother is bleeding me dry."

"Geez, I'm not here for money. I just have a question."

"Okay, well, why don't you sit here, then?" He patted the worn, blue cushion on the wooden chair, then he sat in the wicker rocking chair next to it.

His hair had silvered considerably and he looked weary, not from work or the day but from life. I fumbled with the triskele in my dress's pocket and attempted to form what I needed to say, but he broke the silence.

"So, it's been a while. What brings you here today?"

I breathed in deep to fill my lungs and took the plunge. "I have a question about your blood type."

His face furrowed and he tapped his foot while he rocked. "You're not having health problems, are you?"

"No, no. Nothing of the sort. Your blood type is O if I remember correctly?"

"Sure is." He patted his chest three times. "My blood is so outstanding I'm a universal donor."

"Well, my blood type came back as AB at a blood drive this morning."

He stiffened and turned his face away from me.

"If your blood is type O—" I lumbered forward and almost choked on the knot in my throat. "—and Mother has A, then mine should be either A or O, but it isn't."

"Jesus, Kelly. What do you want from me?"

"All I want is the truth. I think I deserve that much."

He was quiet for a few minutes, then out of nowhere, he rambled, "I did the best I could, you know. Your mother, she had a wild streak in her when we met and thought she'd settle down. When she found out she was pregnant with you, something just didn't sit right, and then you were born with blue eyes. You can go back to the stone age in my bloodline and there's never been blue eyes. I wanted to forget it, to put it behind me, but every God damn time I looked at you, I saw another man's face, some one night stand's permanent mistake."

I sat up straight with a start. "I'm a mistake? One

night stand?"

"Poor choice of words." He cleared his throat. "Your mother went to a concert with Charlene and acted very off for weeks afterward. My gut told me something happened at that concert, but she wouldn't discuss it." He closed his eyes and lowered the volume of his voice. "After I saw your eyes, Diana admitted she got rip-roaring drunk at the concert and slept with some guy in his van. She swore up and down it would be the last time she'd stray or drink, and I think she held true to both promises. But none of that matters anymore."

I felt like someone smacked me in the face with a skillet, and I found it difficult to breathe. I slowly shook my head back and forth and mumbled through tight lips, "So, do you know who my biological father is?"

"No, I don't. Diana doesn't, either. She said she never asked for his name, and I believe her."

"Oh, my God," I whispered with the veins in my neck throbbing.

He resumed tapping his foot. "I was selfish and let my bruised pride prevent me from doing the right thing. I was a bastard to you, Kelly, I know I was. Hell, nobody would have ever known I wasn't your father unless Diana or I told them, but if anyone happened to figure it out, I would have been a laughingstock. Your mother, she compensated for her lack of fidelity by attempting to mold you into the perfect child who would do no wrong and never embarrass either of us. But she was embarrassed by you ever since the moment she found out she was pregnant with you."

I nodded to acknowledge I was still listening despite my closed eyes, and he mused, "It's amazing how your perspective changes with age. I should have left your mother and taken Christian and you with me, I know that now, but back then…"

"Back then what?"

"I was raised believing a real man stuck around for the good and the bad, and those years with Diana were the most miserable years of my life. The day I told her to leave, well, that's the day I regained whatever was left of my life, which isn't much. Here I am, near retirement age with no opportunity to retire because of her outrageous alimony payments." He smudged away the generous tears forming in the corners of his eyes. "I'm so sorry, Kelly. I can't change the past. You are doing so well now…if it means anything, you are not a mistake, and I am proud of you."

He was proud of me.

I wept for the second time in a matter of hours, but this go around was considerably different.

"I'm so, so, sorry," he croaked. "I want to be your dad and do it right this time, and I hope you'll let me."

I grasped my triskele as my past and present collided, the life I thought I knew ending. The light in my mind vanished into darkness, then reignited with brighter and more dazzling flames. I sprang up with my face streaked with black mascara and my arms outstretched, and he opened his arms to receive me.

We cried and clutched each other in christening our newfound relationship as Dad and daughter.

Chapter Three

As summer took its last bows, I couldn't wait to be back inside my classroom and once again in the company of my colleagues. I leaped out of bed at four in the morning on the first of September with ferocious excitement, shut off the alarm I didn't need, and hopped into the shower.

I traveled with Dad to Key West for a week in July to visit Christian and Diego and celebrate our reconciliation. By the end of the trip, I was tighter than ever with the man whom I had no biological ties to whatsoever but now proudly referred to as Dad.

The irony.

Christian and Diego took us fishing, and I surprised everyone by hooking the biggest tarpon caught on the charter boat in years. It took almost an hour to reel in the goliath, and Diego held the line when the fish reached the boat while Christian took my picture with it. Excruciating pain swelled up and down my arm muscles, but I fought through it and unhooked the tarpon all by myself. I released it back into the crystal-clear water and it swiftly swam away. The charter captain estimated the fish weighed more than a hundred and thirty pounds and added my photograph with the beast to the "angler wall of fame" adorning the boat's cabin.

Diego teased Christian about still being a tourist, but with Dad's arms holding both of us close as the sun descended below the horizon every night, Christian beamed because our family once again existed, although in a new form.

Wayne declined my invitation to join us in Key West. "You're crazy, Kel, for letting him off the hook. No matter how many times he's apologized for the way he treated you, there's no way I'd ever spend a week with him," he chastised after I made airline reservations.

In all honesty, I invited him more out of obligation than fancy and was glad he stayed home.

I fulfilled my vow to Shannon after my Key West trip and finished reading *Ulysses* with massive help from those two literary guides I checked out from the library. I kept notes about what I wanted to discuss with her, with my number one question being why she found *Ulysses* so appealing. We spoke just a few times on the phone during the summer because of her workload, which ended up being more than she anticipated. Our conversations were brief, but she said she had never been happier despite her heavy schedule.

My one summer shortcoming?

Not writing every day.

Better yet, not writing at all.

The bout of writer's block I suffered at the beginning of summer worsened. Instead of being able to delve in and allow my emotions to pan out on the pages of my journal or my laptop's screen, angst obstructed my creativity and stifled my voice.

The brand new school year gave me fresh hope. I trusted my rigid teaching schedule and my professional responsibilities, which transformed from a blank slate on August thirty-first to a running list filled with a million things to do on September first, would become the ideal detour for my agitated soul. Anticipating the hectic pace of the next ten months ironically provided me with peace of mind.

I entered Waterville High School's cafeteria with a pep in my step for the first meet and greet of the year. The principal's meet and greet programs were thirty-minute sessions with light refreshments prior to the start time of in-service agendas and provided time to chit chat with colleagues we might not see throughout the school day or even the school year, depending on our respective schedules. I sought out Waterville's three new teachers right away to welcome them with hospitality the same way Shannon greeted me last year when I strode into my first meet and greet replete with intimidation and insecurity.

I spread food service no-brand butter on a cinnamon and raisin bagel wishing it was Kerrygold, then as I reached for an empty cup, I knocked Al's bagel off his plate by mistake and it landed face down on the floor. He grumbled, "You're still a clumsy clod," and skulked away without picking it up.

As Shannon would say, what a douche. I threw the bagel into the garbage can and used a napkin to wipe the residual cream cheese off the floor. Just then, Monica came running over to me with her arms outspread and yodeled, "Kelllleeee, welcome back to the Stingray Pool." She hugged me before passing me on to Del.

"Kelly, baby, wonderful to see you. And check it out, no more wheelchair or crutches," Del boomed then unabashedly yanked up her skirt to expose two rows of zipperlike scars on her leg as if they were medals of honor. I scanned the room in search of Shannon and spotted Dan standing by himself against the furthermost wall, crossed armed and eagle eyeing the door.

At Monica's suggestion, we shared the best part of our summer and I spoke about reconciling with Dad despite learning he wasn't my biological father. Del put her arm around me and said, "Wow, chickee. Pretty intense story. You should write a book about it someday."

"Maybe I will, Del." I nodded. "Maybe I will."

The principal announced the first session of the day would start soon, and a line of teachers snaked from the cafeteria to the auditorium with the English department bringing up the rear. A hand clasped the nape of my neck and a familiar voice from behind instructed, "Last row, Kel."

I almost didn't recognize Shannon with new blonde highlights painted on her ginger tresses. She guided me to her chosen row and happily jabbered, "I had the most amazing summer of my life."

Dan creeped up from behind and grouched, "Boy, Moran, I didn't think you could be more of a whore, but your new hair style certainly proves me wrong."

Shannon tensed and retorted, "One more time, Dan, and I'm going to our affirmative action officer."

"Whatever." He plodded down the slope of the auditorium to the front row and plopped into the seat next to Al just as the principal requested everyone's attention.

Shannon drew a green heart on my agenda, and I wrote underneath it, "finished *Ulysses*." She nudged me with her elbow and whispered, "We'll talk later."

The day was jam packed with meetings and frenzied scrambling to finish as much classroom decorating, planning, and photocopying as possible during the few schedule breaks. With just one more in-service day before students reported for their first day of school, there was no way I would make any sort of dent in my to-do list unless I stayed late. I telephoned Wayne at three to let him know I'd still be a few hours, and after I left a message on the machine, I wondered why I even bothered.

I arranged my classroom desks into pods of four instead of rows to try something different. As I positioned the last desk, I overheard Shannon warn, "I told you, I've had enough of your antics, Dan. I swear I'll press harassment charges if you don't cease and desist."

His strident footsteps echoed between the metal lockers and cinderblock walls, and once the coast was clear, I stuck my head sideways through Shannon's doorway and posed, "You okay?"

"Your crooked Kilroy gets me every time." She giggled and chucked a crumpled piece of paper into the waste basket. "Yes, I'm okay. My attorney advised me to notify both her and administration if Dan continues to harass me, and if he knows what's good for him, he'll stop with his shenanigans. Now's a great time to catch up if you don't mind lending a hand with my bulletin boards." She held out a handful of bright pre-cut borders. "I should have come in earlier to work on setting up my classroom, but…" Her voice trailed off.

"But what?"

Shannon brandished the borders, and their glitter made them shimmer like sequins. "Never mind. Want to help?"

"Sure. Let's take down the faded bulletin board paper first. You've got plenty of new paper on the green roll over there."

"You're right. Wasn't I the one doling out bulletin board advice at this time last year?"

"Yes, you were. I can't believe how fast the year flew by."

Shannon measured the clover-shaded paper then cut enough for the three boards. I held the first sheet up while she stapled it to the cork and said, "So, tell me about your summer. You finished *Ulysses*, and we'll get to Joyce soon enough. What did you write this summer?"

"Nothing," I blurted out.

She frowned and dropped the stapler, which clunked loudly on the tile floor. "Nothing? Why not?"

"The words, I don't know, they just dried up since our first day off in June, then after the issues with my Dad…"

"What issues?"

"Oh, I didn't tell you. I came to the June blood drive and found out my blood type was different than what I thought. Turns out my Dad is not my biological father."

"Holy shit, Kelly, for real?"

"Yes. We talked things out, and I made peace with him. We even traveled together to Key West for a week to visit my brother."

Shannon raised her eyebrow and deadpanned toward me. "Let me get this straight. This man, who by your own admission did nothing to intervene when your mother treated you like an animal, you not only forgave him, but voluntarily spent time with him? You're a better person than I am. I would have told him to go to hell."

"Wayne said the same thing, but the truth is, I'm sick and tired of running away. Sometimes, water is thicker than blood, and by burying the hatchet, I can allow his ocean to combine with my sea and we can be a part of each other's life. As for my mother, she'll remain dead to me."

"So, your real father, do you know who he is?"

"No. Dad said she was drunk and cheated on him with some nameless hookup at a concert."

"Your mother is a real prize," Shannon balked.

"She's the worst, I know. I picked up a part-time hostess shift at the Deck as a diversion to maintain whatever sanity I had left. Dom's such a great person, and just being with him a few hours every day helped me ignore my loss of fluency and forget about the fact I don't know squat about my biological father."

"Maybe it's him," she snorted.

"Oh, God." I laughed out loud. "I'd actually be fine with that, but Dom's never been to a concert in his life."

"And Wayne? Things any better there?"

"Not really. Working at Dom's also allowed me to turn a blind eye to Wayne's drunken antics. He'll never change, and I'm an idiot for thinking he would." I shivered. "Let's change the subject."

"Good idea. It's *Ulysses* time. What did you think?" Shannon held the paper up against the last board while I took over the stapling duties.

"I finished it, even though I had to use two books from the library to help me understand what I read. Tell me, why do you like *Ulysses* so much?"

"It's Joyce, and it's set in Dublin," she replied matter-of-factly.

I crossed my arms and chided in humor, "Really, Shannon?"

She glided her hand over the freshly hung green paper. "Even though the main character is Leopold Bloom, you remember Stephen Dedalus from *Portrait* I

hope, how he was a teacher but wanted
said before, to me, Stephen is you. I am c
you had such difficulty writing this summ
reading *Ulysses* would have summoned the wor
you, not suffocate them. If I ever thought it woul
had the opposite effect, I never would have sugges
you read it."

I held up posters one at a time and Shannon stapled them into place. "It's not your fault. The book is not the cause of my writer's block." The next poster featured a quote from *Ulysses*.

"Isn't this ironic?" I chuckled.

Shannon read it aloud. "To learn one must be humble. But life is the great teacher." She took a deep breath and explained, "*Ulysses,* the entire book takes place on one single day and documents one man's walk about Dublin. Leopold Bloom is a different kind of hero than Odysseus or Beowulf because he's an everyman, like you and me. The most ordinary moments throughout his day are absolutely extraordinary, yet he doesn't realize it. None of us do. Cherish the moments at hand, the little things throughout your day, Kel. That's Joyce's message. The ordinary is extraordinary, and life will eventually teach you every lesson you need to learn."

I silently ruminated about what Shannon said as she continued, "Ever since I first read Joyce, I believed the only place in the world where I could be my best self was Dublin, like when I finally made it there, that's where the real 'me' would flourish and shine. But you know what? I can do just that right here in Waterville. I'm going to teach from my heart, learn as much as possible from my classes, and live the crap out of every single moment because life is too damn short. Then, when my feet

ow Leopold's and Stephen's and Joyce's in Dublin
xt summer, I'll come to the pinnacle of my journey as
 e most authentic and complete version of myself."

"So far," I interrupted. "Your journey so far."

"Speaking of far—" She hiked up the leg of her jeans to unveil a recently-inked purple butterfly tattoo just above her right ankle knob. "—how's this for something far out?"

"The artwork is beautiful, Shannon."

"A permanent reminder of how the caterpillar metamorphosed into the butterfly, I am transforming into who I'm meant to be."

I gazed through the windows at the sun declining in the west and said, "I haven't had many close friends. I'm glad we have each other."

Shannon joined me at the window and clasped her hand in mine. "Me too, Kel. Friends forever."

We watched the barn swallows dodge the dragonflies as their late afternoon competition of diving for insects commenced over the practice fields.

****

Lesson planning, grading, testing, and school traditions filled the frenzied autumn and left me with little time for anything else, including writing. I immersed myself even deeper in the Waterville pool with my students my top priorities, although my luster for teaching a tad dimmer than last year. The revolution of school, prepping, home, dinner, planning, and sleep, except for Fridays when I swung by Delancy's, came to be automatic.

But the more I worked, the more Wayne drank.

Our relationship eroded day after day, and Wayne started crashing at Ed's more nights than not following a mid-October blowout. He held firm to his belief that since he paid the bills, he should be able to live his life however he wanted. I pointed out he didn't pay the bills but his inheritance did and offered to pay for household expenses in place of depositing my paycheck into a separate savings account at his insistence.

Nothing was resolved, and the cycle of disconnection continued.

Shannon and I had different planning and lunch periods, and with her free time consumed with work for her online classes, there was little opportunity for face-to-face interactions. We checked in a few times a day via messages, but emails and texts were not the same as spending time with her in person.

I missed her.

My autumn differed greatly from last year. It was long and lonely instead of intriguing and exhilarating, and my loss of words further intensified my disenchantment.

I woke one morning in early November to several bizarre text messages from Shannon waiting for me on my phone, something about big news. I shot off a quick reply of just a question mark then got ready for school. When I pulled into the staff lot at six fifteen, Shannon's black coupe was already parked in the front row.

She was never at school this early, at least not since I started teaching at Waterville.

I rushed into the building and spied her through her classroom door's thin window sitting with her head on her arms and her red mane cascading over the side of her desk. I jiggled the doorknob and gently knocked.

"Shannon? It's me."

She lifted her head with a start, and I assumed she

had been crying by her red and puffy eyes.

"Let me in, please," I pleaded.

She rose slowly, rubbed her eyes, and shuffled to the door. She unlocked it and muttered, "Hey, you. Sorry I'm so out of it." She dragged her feet back to her desk.

I dropped my school satchel and lunch box in front of the room and said, "Okay, fess up. What is going on? What's the big news?"

Shannon took a gulp of her black coffee then groggily mumbled, "What are you talking about?"

"You sent me these last night." I handed her my phone.

She read her own words from the text thread she sent me near midnight, "At Delancy's. Big news, major big, the future."

"Oh, God," she groaned and laid her head back down while shielding her eyes. "I want to crawl into a cave and stay there forever."

"You'll be okay"—I smoothed her hair—"just pull yourself together and the last bell of the day will be ringing before you know it."

"Screw it all. My hair's fine. The problem is my hand."

"What do you mean? Did you injure it somehow?" I wriggled her hands with mine, but she resisted. "Just show me already."

Shannon took her left hand out from under the desk. The gleaming ring adorning her left ring finger almost blinded me with its center glittering diamond as big as a blueberry and surrounded by emeralds and smaller diamonds. "Congratulations, Shannon!" I jumped up and down and yelped, which made her cringe. I froze and asked, "This isn't good news?"

She lumbered to the whiteboard to write her agenda for the day but hastily recapped the blue marker with a wave of green passing over her face. "The smell of these markers is going to make me hurl."

"Spill it. There's more going on here than just a hangover."

She placed her newly-ringed hand on her stomach. "Well, suffice it to say last night will be the last time I'll party for the next eight or nine months."

"No!" I inhaled sharply and covered my mouth with my hand.

Shannon's upper lip quivered. "There goes my Dublin dream, Kel. I finally had all my ducks in a row, but there's no way I'll be able to study in Ireland while caring for an infant. You're the only one besides Oliver who knows about the baby, so please don't tell anyone."

The rumble of students flooding the hallways vibrated through the floor. I seized her two shoulders with my hands and ordered, "You've got to get yourself together. Drink lots of water and do your job. We'll figure everything out later."

Shannon sulked. "I guess I can do this."

"You can, and you will."

I jostled to my classroom and scribbled an agenda on the board then took my post at the doorway to welcome my first period students. I nodded. "Good morning Ronnie, Hannah, Shauna."

Joyful cheers emerged from Shannon's classroom just after the morning bell rang, with a voice yelling over the noise, "You're engaged, Miss Moran?"

"Yes, I'm going to be Mrs. O'Shea," Shannon sang before a voice over the intercom interjected and requested everyone to rise for the Pledge of Allegiance.

Sounded like she bounced back after putting on her teacher mask. My thoughts shifted to Dan, and I prayed he would remain civil once word reached him about Shannon's impending marriage to Oliver, and eventually, the baby.

After the morning announcements ended, my students, buzzing with curiosity, assaulted me with a barrage of questions. "Did Miss Moran really get engaged? When's her wedding? Tell us about your wedding. I'm going to have a cake made from cupcakes and a chocolate fountain at my wedding."

I gave my students the evil eye and lightheartedly reprimanded, "Boy, you are very interested in something not at all related to what our good friend, Mister Macbeth, will do today, so let's open our books to page 303. I'll answer all your questions once we finish reading Act One and complete our daily writing reflection." The class groaned in unison while I assigned the day's reading roles.

During my planning period, Monica yodeled my name from behind me in the hallway. I turned around just as she dropped her stack of papers, and they floated in all directions to blanket the floor. "Did you hear the great news?" she gushed. "Shannon and Oliver are engaged. I'm so thrilled I can't even hold on to my essays."

I bent down to help her clean up the mess and flatly replied, "Yes, I did."

"You don't sound very excited about it." A grimace replaced the joy on Monica's face.

"It's exciting news for sure. I just slept like garbage last night, plus I have to make copies before next period, and Al's probably hogging the copier," I fibbed.

The mailroom was abuzz with the news of

Shannon's engagement when we entered. Al motioned me to the copier and said, "Almost done. Send your job through so it starts after mine finishes."

I raised my eyebrow and replied, "Thanks, Al."

His gallantry was short lived. "So, I hear Shannon's engaged? She'll regret it."

"I beg your pardon?" I snapped.

"Dan's a much better guy than Oliver the chump."

"Quit stirring a pot that is not on your stove." I inadvertently interrupted my copy job by hitting a button with my flailing arm and groaned out loud.

Monica came from behind and cackled, "Isn't it great news about Shannon, Al?"

"Whatever. She'll be a bitch no matter whose last name she takes, just like this one here." He motioned his head toward me and shirked out of the mailroom.

Monica frowned. "What's wrong with him?"

"Side effects of being a giant ass, I presume. I'll see you later, okay? I've got to telephone a parent."

I returned to my classroom and stared out of the center window, my attention fixated on the gym classes essentially going nowhere as they walked laps around the circular track.

****

I stood by Shannon's side as a bridesmaid when Miss Moran became Mrs. O'Shea eight days later at Waterville Town Hall during a much smaller wedding than the grandiose affair she fantasized about since she was a little girl.

"I now pronounce you husband and wife. You may kiss your bride," the officiant's voice resounded through the courtroom.

The guests applauded the newlyweds as they

exchanged their first married kiss, and on the recession out, I picked up Shannon's sunflower bouquet Deirdre dropped by mistake. Shannon's cascading, white veil blew in the breeze and netted a few brown and yellow leaves as she descended the town hall steps while holding Oliver's hand. My gaze followed the veil's trail between the two bouquets I carried, and I did a double take.

I spied Dan snooping from the alleyway. He wore a University of New Jersey baseball cap and a throwback brown bomber jacket recycled from two decades ago. I lowered the flowers just as he removed his aviator sunglasses, and when his eyes met mine, he quickly retreated in the opposite direction. I distracted Shannon so she would not notice him. "Let me see your ring one more time, Shannon." The newlyweds stuck out their ringed hands for another obligatory "just married check out our wedding rings" photo.

We paraded in a group three doors down to The Ardmore for the reception under Dan's surveillance I'm sure, but I didn't spot him anywhere. As everyone else filed into the smaller of the two ballrooms, the bride and I darted into the ladies' room.

Shannon touched up her makeup with sheer bliss emanating from her cheekbones. "I didn't think I was ready for any of this, and I was devastated at having to abandon my Dublin dream. But you know what, Kelly? I am really happy. I did the right thing by marrying Oliver. I love that son of a bitch so much, and this little one too." She patted her belly.

"What a great attitude." I leaned in so we were cheek to cheek and draped my right arm over her shoulder. "Check out our reflection in the mirror. We've got to tell the photographer to take a picture of us posing like this."

We both beamed, and she took my right hand in hers. "I couldn't have done any of this without you."

"My pleasure, Mrs. O'Shea."

Deirdre burst into the bathroom with a scowl on her face and her small arms flailing wildly, like one of those blowups commonly seen at used car lots. She bellowed at her sister, "What's the hold up? Everyone is waiting for you."

I adjusted Shannon's veil on the way to the happy hour area, and she made her grand entrance whooping, "Let's get this party started!"

Oliver hurried over with two shot glasses of ginger ale and gushed, "Here's to my bride, the love of my life." Shannon snatched both and downed them one after the other. Oliver laughed as he cheerfully chastised her, "One of those was for your husband, you know."

It might not have been the way she envisioned getting married, but Shannon's small reception was absolutely spectacular, with delicious food and Del the ringleader of the dance floor. She so successfully cajoled guests to boogie during every song, the DJ offered her a part-time job as his assistant.

My wistful psyche soon got the better of me, and I needed a reprieve from the riotous music and heavy air. I stepped outside into the brisk November wind to gather my thoughts when the faint notes from a familiar song emanated from the wedding in the larger ballroom.

I plugged my left ear with my finger and leaned in the music's direction to listen closer, then I cringed when I recognized it as the song I did not remember swaying with Wayne to in the middle of the street on our own drunken wedding night, the song he dubbed our wedding song.

The whole new world I counted on with Wayne didn't exist.

Blinded by booze for years, I mistakenly believed in it, just as I wrongly believed in him and in us. Once I eliminated the alcohol from my side of the equation, the glaring reality about our sham of a marriage shone crystal clear, but I denied it over and over.

The bitter truth smacked me across my face—my husband and I had grown so apart he couldn't even accompany me to my best friend's wedding.

As the music shifted to that classic, opening riff made famous by The Sopranos finale, I trembled and confided to the full moon, "This small-town girl doesn't know what to believe in anymore."

****

I broke tradition and accepted Dad's invitation to Thanksgiving dinner at The Hurricane over in Oldentown Beach, which boasted a five-course buffet feast complete with all the traditional holiday fixings.

Wayne was…how should I say it?

Displeased.

Yes, displeased.

In fact, he was so displeased I chose dinner with Dad over going to Moira's with him and whomever her tail of the month happened to be, he didn't come home the night before Thanksgiving. Since staying out developed into his modus operandi, I shouldn't have been surprised

But this time, something felt different.

Different and foreboding.

Every single cell in my body sensed something wasn't right.

I tossed and turned all night, courtesy of the loud and

menacing delusions spinning in my mind. As night segued to morning, I showered and fixed myself an unsatisfying cup of coffee then channel surfed in the Smuggler's room when the front door slammed out of nowhere.

"Kelly! Kelly!" Wayne's boisterous voice reverberated throughout the townhouse.

I dashed to the kitchen and found him standing with a puddle forming on the tile floor underneath him. His sea glass blues were gray, frosted and intimidating instead of clear and enchanting.

"Happy Thanksgiving?" I said with apprehension. "Why are you soaking wet?"

"It's pouring outside," he snarled.

"Okay, but that doesn't explain why you're screaming my name like a banshee."

"This is it!" He punched his fist into the air and roared, "I'm leaving for good unless you give me a reason to stay."

My heart launched into my throat, and I floundered to form a coherent response in my pounding head. Wayne misinterpreted my silence, which agitated him further. "Mom was right. I deserve a wife who wants to have fun with me, not someone who puts her shit job and her shit students and her shit writing in front of me. This marriage is over."

He stamped into the bedroom and yammered incoherently while he ripped open and banged shut dresser drawers and closet doors. My mind was in a flurry yet stalled at the same time. I couldn't figure out what to do or what to say and just stood there like an imbecile. Wayne stormed back into the kitchen wearing dry jeans and a black t-shirt with his facial muscles twitching like crazy. He carried his winter coat, a duffel bag full of his clothes, and his sneakers.

"Calm down a minute, Wayne. Let's talk." I slid one of the high-top chairs out for him, but he kicked it over and glared at me, his icy countenance sending trembles down my back.

"It's too late. Even if we talk, nothing will change. You'll be involved in some bullshit basket weaving club or whatever other excuse you can think of for staying late at school. I'll be left alone as usual, my wife working even though she doesn't have to, not here to cook me dinner or clean up like a good wife should."

Something festered inside me as I countered, "Whoa, Wayne, now hold it right there. Where exactly is this coming from?"

"Mom said for years I deserve better, that marrying you was a mistake, and she's right. You hold me back, and I've been too blind to see it until now."

A furor like I never experienced before flooded my body. "You are preposterous. I hold you back? From what? You don't do a Goddamn thing. I can't believe you have the audacity to blame me for your lot in life, you son of a bitch."

"You don't want to be with me, so fuck you, Kelly. Fuck you and your entire pathetic existence. I'll be back tomorrow to get the rest of my shit." He thundered out of the townhouse like a cyclone and slammed the door behind him so hard the wedding picture of us drunk at city hall fell off the wall, its glass frame smashing to pieces.

I couldn't move.

My feet felt like they were literally bolted to the floor.

How could he?
Scratch that.
How dare he?
I hold him back?
He has held me back since the day we met, dammit, and his weight has fallen on me for far too long.

I clenched my fists tighter and tighter and tore to the Smuggler's room. I scanned the room with hot eyes, seized a pillow, and screamed as loud as I could into it, then pummeled it over and over and imagined it gushing blood from the force of my fist. The pillow tumbled to the floor, and I kicked it so hard it knocked my laptop to the ground.

My eye caught my silhouette in the mural.

What a stupid, idiotic girl, sitting there dreaming and writing and wasting her life.

I punched my likeness so hard she disappeared forever into the sheetrock, then I plunged onto the bed back first, my chest exploding as I gasped for air.

I held my swollen and throbbing right hand with my left and rolled over onto my side. My wrecked laptop lay reduced to pieces on the wood floor, a victim of my frenzy, and everything I didn't back up now lost for good. One lone tear seeped from my eye, followed by another. Incapacitated with a despair so extreme, I could barely breathe as the laments viciously emerged from my body.

My thoughts turned to the last time such a hopelessness overwhelmed me, and my chest rose and fell with heavy breaths as part of me wished for that blue bottle. I vehemently rejected the fleeting idea of the light supposedly shining ahead of me.

The harsh truth was there was nothing shining ahead

of me.

Absolutely nothing at all.

I closed my eyes and silently counted to one hundred while pushing the idea of the permanent escape lurking near the border of sanity in my mind a little further away with every number forward.

My panting slowly subsided and my breath restored to normal, but there was nothing normal about how I felt.

I retrieved my triskele and grasped the trinket in my fist while the ceiling fan's blurred blades hypnotized me. If Shannon wasn't at her aunt's helping prepare Thanksgiving dinner, I would have called her.

My cell phone buzzed, and I flatly mumbled into its receiver, "Hello?"

"Hi, Kelly." I could hear the concern in Dad's voice. "Are you still coming for dinner?"

"Yeah, sorry I'm running late." I spoke in a more upbeat tone to hide the truth. "I'll be there in a few."

I hung up and tried to improve my rumpled appearance, but makeup couldn't conceal my swollen cheeks or my bloodshot eyes. I slid my head through the neck of my brown and orange knee-length dress, gathered my hair in a bun, knotted my scarf scattered with pumpkins at my neck, and yanked on my brown suede boots.

Then I drove like the dickens to The Hurricane.

Dad was already seated at a table for two, and as I advanced, his smile transformed into a frown. I gave him a nimble peck on the forehead, and he asked, "Kelly, are you okay?"

"Yeah, just marital problems."

"If I've learned anything, it's that life is too short for the bullshit."

"You speak the truth. I'm glad we're together for Thanksgiving dinner this year, Dad."

"Me too. It's what I'm most grateful for, the fact I have my daughter back." He winked at me. The server took our drink order then clarified the procedures for the buffet. After he left, Dad kidded, "Does he really think we don't know what we're doing, that we're buffet nubes?"

His joke made me laugh notwithstanding the dense fog between my ears. Over dinner, we chatted about Christian's new art commission for a mural at the Key West Visitors Center. Dad asked me about my life, and I told him about going back to school and what it was like to be a teacher, but neither of us mentioned married life or our spouses.

Even though we were both stuffed, we each made two trips to the dessert table for pumpkin pie once our server brought coffee. Dad chuckled at how much whipped cream I piled on top of mine and said, "It's uncanny we share an affinity for whipped cream and butter."

He handed me a card when we said farewell in the parking lot. "Read it when you get home, kiddo. Happy Thanksgiving, Kelly."

"Happy Thanksgiving, Dad."

He kissed my cheek, and we parted ways.

With the range of the day's emotions leaving me spent, I craved the comfort of the real Smuggler's and soon parked facing the current. Although it was dark outside, I could clearly visualize the waves and the movement of the water just by the sounds emanating from the inlet. The sea's distinct smell soothed me as soon as I inhaled it.

I ripped open the envelope from Dad and removed a simple Thanksgiving card with a cartoon turkey under a "Count Your Blessings" heading. His scrawled handwriting filled the interior.

The only thing outweighing my guilt of hurting you for years is my love for you, Kelly. On this Thanksgiving, I am most grateful for your forgiveness and for finally having a daughter. You and Christian are my biggest blessings. With love, Dad.

I whispered, "I love you, Dad."

A swarm of cars filled with screaming teenagers barreled into the lot and ended my peace.

It was time to go home, and the possibilities of what might be waiting there terrified me.

I guardedly unlocked and nudged open the front door, then breathed a sigh of relief at no sign of Wayne. I wormed into a pair of fleece pants and a black Waterville High School sweatshirt and wondered if Wayne would come home or not, and if he did, if he would provoke another altercation.

I elected to sleep on the living room sofa because I wouldn't have to see my smashed computer or the hole I punched into my mural twin. Plus, if Wayne did show up, I'd hear him instantly. As the last football game of the day kicked off, I nestled on the couch with my blanket and pillow, then when my eyelids became heavy, I lowered the volume and fell right asleep.

A thunderous banging frightened me awake near midnight, my disorientation confounded by the unfamiliarity of sleeping in the living room.

I rubbed my face and heard the noise again, a strident thumping from outside.

Someone was pounding on the door.

I hurried over in a daze and flung it open to find two Waterville police officers instead of Ed propping up Wayne.

"Good evening," the officer on the left addressed me through his stoic countenance. "Are you Kelly Coopersmith?"

"I'm Kelly Lynch," I answered with caution as my legs started to tremble. "Wayne Coopersmith is my husband."

The officers regarded each other and the one on the left continued, "I'm Officer Robinson. This is Officer Webber. We know it's late, but we need to talk with you. May we please come in?"

"Of course. Have a seat on the couch." I sat on the recliner with the two officers facing me and braced for it.

Officer Robinson's voice shattered the thick silence. "I'm afraid we have some terrible news. Your husband, Wayne, was struck by two vehicles on The Boulevard earlier tonight and was killed instantly."

"What?" I gasped, my stomach feeling like it was dropping from the peak of the world's tallest roller coaster. "This has to be a mistake. He was at Moira's…"

"I'm very sorry but it's not a mistake."

Sobs built up behind my eyes. "But…I thought he…he was with Ed."

This was not happening.

Officer Webber continued, "Someone named Ed Rossman attempted to subdue him, but your husband broke free and ran right in front of a pickup truck traveling in the westbound lane. The truck hit him and the impact caused him to fly into the air and he landed in the eastbound lane where another car drove over him.

The accident investigation is still continuing, but it's doubtful charges will be filed against either driver because neither had time to avoid hitting him."

Officer Robinson interjected, "Because you are his spouse, we need you to identify his body at the morgue."

The pall of the officers' words hung in the air, stinking and raw.

Identify his body? How could this be real?

"You already know it's him," I bawled. "I don't want to see him all mangled."

Officer Webber cleared his throat. "I understand how difficult this is for you, but it's police procedure because he did not have any identification on him. Mr. Rossman is at the station, and we will arrange for him to meet us at the hospital morgue. If he provides the visual identification of Wayne's cadaver and you agree with him, that will suffice."

Cadaver.

Wayne was now considered a cadaver.

I could barely see either officer through my tears. I stammered, "Can I...bring a friend...Shannon with me?"

"Yes. Have her meet us at the hospital."

In a haze, I numbly fumbled to locate Shannon's phone number and dialed two wrong numbers by mistake before I got it right.

Shannon answered in a drowsy voice, "Well, this better be good."

"Shan, it's me, Kelly, and I need you," I wailed. "Wayne's dead, hit by a car. Can you meet me at the hospital?"

I heard Shannon scrambling. "What? Holy shit, Kel. I'm on my way."

I threw on my coat, grabbed my wallet, and shuffled

in a stupor out to the squad car between the officers. Officer Robinson sped the whole way to Waterville General Hospital with the car's revolving blue and red lights bouncing off everything we passed.

Shannon sprinted over to me in front of the emergency room entrance. "Oh my God, Kelly."

I grasped her tight and blubbered, "You were the first person I thought to call."

"I'm here, Kel. It's okay, I'm here."

"I didn't think, is the baby okay?"

"Yes, don't worry. Everything's fine."

We followed the officers through the lobby to the elevator, then into the hallway of the basement morgue. Ed sat on a wooden bench with new wounds on his elbows and the side of his face, and blood splatters on his jeans and work boots. He bawled through his bloated eyes when he saw me, "Kelly, I swear I tried, but I just couldn't keep my grip."

"Ed"—I sobbed and shuddered—"what the hell happened?"

"I don't know, he all of a sudden went berserk in the back of The Rip Tide, yelling something about you deserving better, he'd never be anything more than a drunk and you'd be better off alone—" He gasped for air. "—and I don't know what set him off. He was fine one minute, then a complete lunatic the next. He raced out the door, I tackled him to the ground, but he wrestled free, and bolted right into the street. The truck hit him before I could get to my feet."

He violently sniveled and continued his confession, "I'll never forget the sound...of that truck hitting him...or the sound...of his bones cracking...under the other car. I should have stopped him...I couldn't...but I should have."

I cried.

I just cried.

After what felt like an eternity, Officer Webber spoke. "I understand how emotional this is for all of you, but we need to proceed with the identification process. Please follow me."

Shannon supported me on my right side and Ed held onto my left, and the three of us entered the morgue. The room was as chillingly cold as a dark January day. I shivered and followed Officer Webber to a silver table with a white sheet shrouding an obvious body. I shut my eyes and gripped Shannon's arm so hard my fingernails almost pierced her skin.

Officer Webber asked, "Ms. Lynch, can you positively identify this body as your husband, Wayne Coopersmith?"

I opened my eyes and sucked in my breath as he peeled back the sheet to unveil what was left of Wayne…his blond hair matted with dried blood and small chunks of asphalt…his face, mangled and torn…his right sea glass blue eye relocated to just above his mouth…

His disfigurement sliced straight into my soul.

I shielded my face and whimpered, "Yes. That is my husband, Wayne Coopersmith."

"Thank you. You can go into the hall whenever you're ready," Officer Webber said while pulling the sheet to cover Wayne.

Ed and Shannon guided me back into the hallway just as a woman's piercing scream echoed from inside the stairwell, "I am not waiting for the elevator, dammit!"

A door flew open, and Moira burst into the hallway like a typhoon in red spiked heels and a short red-and-black sequined dress. "You've got my boy, and I demand to see him," she screeched, then she barged toward me. "You. This is your fault, you fucking bitch. You killed my boy. He'd still be alive if it wasn't for you. I'll murder you!" Moira lunged for me but the two officers escorting her held her back.

"Ma'am, do not threaten this young woman again, or I'll be forced to take you into custody," Officer Robinson commanded while Officer Webber shielded me.

"Take me into custody?" Moira screamed. "She's the one who should be locked up because she killed my son." She whirled in the clutches of the officers, thrashed her legs in all directions, then stretched her arm for Officer Robinson's gun. He tased her, and she dropped like a sack of potatoes onto the cold, concrete floor.

****

My phone endlessly buzzed with text messages notwithstanding the early hour before I even arrived home to the townhouse.

"I thought only good news was supposed to travel fast. Give me your damn phone," Shannon griped and set it to mute.

I flopped onto the couch, and she took my hand in hers. We sat in silence until my eyes welled up. "I can't believe he's gone, Shan. We had our problems, including one hell of an argument earlier, but I still loved him. Even now I do."

"I know."

"I can't fucking believe this is happening. This morning, he went ballistic, told me he was leaving me, but I never expected this. I'll never…never gaze into those…sea glass blues…again," I stammered then buried my tear-streaked face into Shannon's shoulder.

"Hold on a sec, he said he was leaving you? Well, that doesn't matter now. I'm so sorry you have to go through this."

The morning's first colors peeked through the eastern sky and reflected onto the living room walls from the kitchen window. I blew my nose and said, "I just realized, today is Black Friday. Shit, Shannon, this is the blackest Friday of all time. What am I supposed to do now?"

"It's going to be okay, Kel. Listen, I'm just going to run home for a few things then I'll be back. Why don't you try getting some sleep?"

I shook my head. "You and the baby need to rest more than I do. Don't worry about coming back."

"Absolutely not. I'm too amped up to sleep right now, anyway. Want me to bring you anything?"

I thought for a minute, then mumbled, "A latte and a double chocolate brownie from The Gutter."

"As you wish. Be back soon."

I putzed around the townhouse in a daze, pacing the same path eight or nine times before I stopped in front of the Smuggler's door. I stood there for either a few minutes or a few hours, who knew since I lost all concept of time.

When my feet were once again able to move, I opened the door, peeked into the room, and stepped over the remnants of my laptop on the carpet then tiptoed over to the hole in the mural. I grazed my bruised right hand over the concave void, then I picked up a small, framed picture from the desk. I took out the photograph of

Wayne taken up at Smuggler's right after we first met, kissed it, then stuffed it in the mural's hole.

Then I collapsed to the floor in paralyzing tremors as the sharp laptop fragments stabbed my side from all directions.

****

The next week was the longest week of my life.

A complete blur.

And complete and utter shit.

My saving grace was Shannon. She prepared my substitute lesson plans since I would be taking bereavement leave the following week. She also picked up Christian and Diego from the airport and coordinated meal drop offs from my Waterville High School family. She even had the foresight to keep a running list of thank you notes I would need to send in time.

I planned a simple memorial service for Wayne at Bolton's Funeral Home. Shannon and Dad sat next to me, with Christian and Diego on Dad's right and Oliver next to Shannon. Ed sat behind me with my principal and two of Wayne's pool buddies and three bartenders from The Rip Tide I never met. Two police officers escorted Moira, who shrieked, "My beautiful son," every few minutes.

I didn't know if I was dreaming, viewing my life on a big screen, or experiencing it firsthand in reality.

When it was time to deliver Wayne's eulogy, Shannon bent toward me and whispered, "You've got this."

I drifted in a daze to the podium at the front of the room and smoothed my pulsating fingertips over Wayne's engraved initials on his pewter urn. "Thank you all for coming today. I never would have thought I'd be standing here under these circumstances"—my body trembled, and I had difficulty reading my own words—"Wayne was…Wayne was…"

"You murdered my son, you gold-digging harlot!" Moira roared and launched for me.

As the police officers attempted to restrain her, Shannon countered, "You're the only gold digger in this room as far as I can see."

"Fuck you!" Moira screamed, then chaos ensued. Dad and Christian stood in front of me to protect me while Shannon grabbed Wayne's urn so it wouldn't be damaged or spilled in the mayhem. The officers eventually overpowered Moira and hauled her outside to a waiting squad car.

"Let's fix the chairs and get them back into rows," Jacques Bolton the funeral director directed, "then Kelly can finish her eulogy."

"No, I can't. Christian, can you do it?" I shook the lined paper on which I wrote the eulogy in the air. I wept into Dad's chest, Christian read the eulogy, and the service concluded.

Everyone filed out, but I lingered at Wayne's urn with Shannon gently stroking my back. After a few minutes, she said, "It's time to go, Kel."

"I know."

She stepped backward, and I bent down to kiss his urn.

"Time for this stage of my life to end," I faltered. "I love you, Wayne."

****

I awoke to a new chapter the following morning, and while I wanted to stay in bed forever, the image of Moira's haggish face in my mind motivated me to get moving. Even though Wayne named me as his sole heir in his will, I didn't trust her as far as I could throw her and feared she'd try to get her claws on his estate. I spent the day with my attorney transferring every household bill, legal document, stock account, and the deed to the townhouse into my name and proceeded with caution everywhere I went because I was terrified of hearing those clicking high heels behind me. That ended, however, when Officer Robinson telephoned to inform me Moira fled to Florida after posting bail and stealing Wayne's urn from Bolton's. He asked me if I wanted to press charges against her for theft of the urn, but I declined.

Wayne belonged with his mother.

I emptied his closet and dressers into black garbage bags to donate but kept his light green surf hoodie still ripe with his comforting scent. I slept with it for a few nights on the couch before I stashed it in the bottom of the bathroom closet.

It took three trips to the local thrift shop to unload his clothing, and after I finished, I second guessed my decision to get rid of everything in such haste.

I could not erase his twisted and injured face from my mind nor shake the feeling I was ultimately responsible for his death. Shannon told me I was being silly, but if it weren't for me and my misguided ambition to better myself by finishing college and becoming a teacher, he'd still be standing next to me. Sure, I'd be as drunk as he was, but that was better than…

It was my fault he died.

I shuffled to the kitchen and opened the refrigerator for a bottle of water. My eyes fell upon the rows of brown bottles with Wayne's poison capped inside, their long necks boring into my mind like drill bits and stinging like peroxide on an open wound. I took each one off the shelves one at a time and created a row on the granite countertop like one in an old western shooting arcade.

As I eyed the lineup, the ache for a taste, just a drop on my tongue from one of the bottles swelled larger as each second passed.

What harm would it do me?

I was going through hell, dammit, and I deserved a way to deal with the fact my husband died because of me.

Because of me.

I snapped off a cap with a bottle opener and breathed in the vapors escaping into the air.

My God, it smelled so freaking good.

I inhaled the ether deep and could taste the amber sweetness that would eliminate my anguish and guilt. I sensed the foamy bubbles teasing the tip of my tongue and the rich smoothness flowing down my throat.

The urge swelled, wild and thick, and I could no longer resist quenching my thirst.

I grasped the bottle in haste, but condensation grew over its exterior like tiny water blisters and it slipped out of my hand just before it touched my lips. It plunged to the floor and splintered into shards while spilling its contents everywhere.

I removed the cap from another, held it for a moment, and dropped it onto the tile, where it exploded.

I cracked the cap off every remaining bottle in succession and let each one plummet to the floor. A lake of lager formed at my feet with its shoreline consisting of cabinet bottoms and broken glass. Both of my sweatpants legs soaked up the beer like a sponge. Once my pants were drenched up to my knees, I precariously hopped toward the hallway and dropped my socks and my pants into the washer.

All of a sudden, the stench made me sick.

I retched in the toilet until my stomach was empty then drained Lake Coopersmith, which included spraying an entire can of lemon-scented freshener to cleanse the air of the swill stench. I mopped, I wrung, and I scrubbed until the kitchen was cleaner than it had been in years.

I showered and changed into a clean hoodie and sweatpants, then closed the door to the Smuggler's room without ever intending to open it again.

****

Shannon visited me a few days later instead of going to Delancy's and brought me a bag of papers from school. While fixing tea for the two of us, she rubbed her belly. "It's nice to see you at ease, Shannon, especially after this week. How are you feeling with the baby and all?"

"The morning sickness finally subsided and I get a little tired, but it's all good. I don't know what I'd do without this little one, here. I treasure her and Oliver even more after witnessing your ordeal with losing Wayne, and she's my reason for living. Dublin will happen in time, and perhaps I'll even have a mini-me travel companion as a bonus."

"You found out it's a girl?"

"No, just a hunch. Your substitute teacher has been great. You have nothing to worry about when you come back to school."

"I'll be there on Monday, which will give me three weeks of teaching before winter break. Geez, I've been so out of it, I forgot Christmas is almost here."

"There's still room for you in the WonderShow cast if you're interested."

"I'd be glad to take on a small part or two."

Shannon abruptly winced and clutched her stomach.

"You all right?" I asked with concern.

"Yeah, I've just been having bouts of pregnancy-related gas the past few days. Excuse me while I use your bathroom before I embarrass myself."

"We all bust ass from time to time, Shan. It's all good."

"Eloquently worded, Kelly." She chuckled before going to the bathroom. I sorted through the contents from my school mailbox, then all of a sudden, Shannon shrieked, "Oh, my God!"

I sprinted to the bathroom door and yelled, "Are you okay?"

"This can't be happening!" she screamed. I forced open the door to find her sitting on the toilet wide-eyed and tremoring. "I'm bleeding, terribly bleeding. Oh God, what do I do?"

I grabbed Wayne's surf sweatshirt from the bottom of the closet thinking it was a towel and commanded, "Put this between your legs. I'm taking you straight to the hospital."

"But…"

"No buts, Shannon. We have to go, now. There's no time to waste."

Hours later, Oliver emerged from the Waterville General Hospital emergency room into the lobby with pink swollen eyes and a despondence I never wanted to witness on anyone's face ever again, including Al the weasel.

"Oliver?" I croaked with a sinking heart.

"The baby's gone."

I fell to the waiting room's sterile couch and sucked in my breath. "Oh, Oliver, I'm so sorry."

"It was a girl," his voice cracked. "Molly. Molly is gone."

We held each other in sorrow, and I asked when he pulled away, "Is Shannon okay?"

"Medically, she's stable, but she's an emotional wreck."

"Can I see her?"

"She doesn't want to see anyone right now. She said she'll call you when she's ready."

"Okay."

Oliver hung his head and shuffled back to the emergency room.

I sat in the waiting area, dejected and pulverized, until an ambulance crew came bursting through in a whirlwind of mayhem with a heart-attack victim.

When I got home, I wrote one passage before slumping on the sofa and enduring another sleepless night—"God, please be with Shannon and comfort her, and please, I beg you, please give me a breather, because I can't handle much more."

****

On my first day back in school in almost two weeks, I entered my classroom to find the whiteboard filled with warm and encouraging sentiments from my students. I read every single word and prepared the day's agenda on posterboard so I wouldn't have to erase the makeshift mural just yet.

A substitute teacher opened Shannon's classroom door, which didn't surprise me. Oliver messaged me that the hospital released her and she would most likely return to school by the end of the week. It killed me I couldn't be there for her, but Oliver relayed it was best to leave her alone for the time being because she was having a very difficult time accepting her miscarriage.

Del and Monica came flying through my classroom door and scooped me up in yodel and song. "No practice for The Show today, but we'll swing by after school to review the script with you," Del said.

I disregarded my distress and stood framed by the doorway, eager to greet my pupils. I never fathomed receiving so many hugs, and of course, I prefaced each one with "hugging in an appropriate way," which made them laugh. I spent my planning period catching up with my fellow Stingrays, even Al, who cordially extended his hand to me and muttered, "Sorry for your loss, Kelly."

My presence inside my second home did wonders for my soul. I desperately needed the diversion from my grief, but Shannon's absence triggered an unwanted anxiety. Del and Monica gave me a hand after school with trimming my room for the holidays and reviewing The Show's details. I would be in the opening number like last year and background in the three classroom skits. I was happy I didn't have to memorize any lines because my brain felt like it was made of mush.

The following morning, the same substitute wrote the day's assignment on Shannon's whiteboard. I texted Shannon another —*Here if you need me*— message, which went unanswered. Del called an emergency meeting of the Welcome Saturnalia WonderShow cast after school, where she shared the news that Shannon would be out until January as per administration. A row promptly began, and after Del announced she'd be taking over as this year's director, I ducked into the hallway to telephone Shannon.

"Shan, it's me." I spoke to her voicemail. "I miss you, and I'm concerned. Please call me back because I'm worried sick about you."

As I climbed into bed, Shannon finally texted me.
—*Hey, you. Just not ready to see or talk yet.*—
I wrote, —*Even me?*—
—*Yes. Someday, I'll explain. I still love you, my friend.*—

It was like a broken record every day—I called or texted both Shannon and Oliver with little to no replies. After seeing my messages on Shannon's phone, Deirdre contacted me to let me know Shannon was seeing a mental health professional to cope with the baby's loss.

In a shocking twist, word filtered through the Waterville staff the day before The Show that Dan submitted his resignation, effective immediately, and he packed his belongings and left New Jersey. He didn't tell anyone the reason for his quick exodus, but the ship of gossip fodders with Al at the helm questioned the paternity of Shannon's lost baby, which by now was common knowledge.

I marched over to Al and his minions after show practice and retaliated, "Knock this off, all of you. Shannon was not having an affair with Dan. She had a miscarriage and is absolutely crushed. You are making everything worse by instigating baseless rumors." The principal then demanded the group of blabbermouths report at once to his office, me not included.

After school, I drove over to Shannon's and knocked for almost ten minutes with no answer even though

Oliver's car was parked on the street and Shannon's was in the driveway. An hour later, Shannon texted, —*Hey, you. Love you.*—

—*Love you too,*— I replied.

Del held her own and directed one hell of a WonderShow, yet I couldn't shake feeling very removed from everyone, the spirit of community and jolliness I experienced last year replaced by distress and melancholy.

I dodged the traditional Stingray welcome-to-winter-break pandemonium at Delancy's and headed straight to Smuggler's instead, where I reread Shannon's last text —*Hey, you. Love you.*—

It was low tide, and despite the lingering stench and the freezing temperature, I ventured onto the jetty where I used to write. The chilly wind soothed me and I allowed the salt air to frolic in my lungs. I trusted my plan of doing absolutely nothing over winter break would revive my soul and revitalize my being.

An inexplicable force from deep within compelled me to rip the triskele I found there so long ago from my pocket. It stared at me while burning my palm, the infernal bauble, and ridiculed me something terrible.

I shouted into the void, "Where the hell is the light that's supposed to be shining ahead of me, anyway?" then bent my arm backward and heaved the talisman with as much strength as I could muster into the outgoing current.

Part Two: The Present, or Death

"His soul swooned slowly as he heard the snow falling faintly through the universe and faintly falling, like the descent of their last end, upon all the living and the dead."

James Joyce, "The Dead"

Ten days to do absolutely nothing…this break is just what I need.

It's cold outside, and I mean, it's frigging cold. The low temperature with its Siberia-like bite has shattered statewide weather records almost every day. While I want to remain burrowed under my cozy blankets, my pantry and refrigerator shelves are bare so I have no choice but to venture out into the tundra.

All I've done is binge football and hockey games and a ton of terrible movies during this self-perpetuated isolation. I haven't written or read a single word except for the sports crawler at the bottom of the television screen. Both my laptop and a bag filled with ungraded essays remain untouched, and it's a safe bet they will stay closed until school resumes next week.

Dad invited me to go down to Key West with him to celebrate Christmas and the arrival of the new year at Christian's, but I can't deal with the hassles of traveling.

And speaking of New Year's, I just want this dreadful year to be over and done with. I should be celebrating its departure with bells on, but I'll most likely be asleep by nine. Like an idiot, I'll drink the "new year, new you" juice when I wake up on January first and expect life to instantaneously transform into a magical fairy tale, but it won't.

It never does.

Anyway, I dash into the Food King and scuff my boots against the black rubber mat just inside of the automatic doors. As I steady my balance in a tightrope-walker manner, a kid standing near the produce laughs at me.

Nothing like making a grand entrance.

Had I taken a spill, my heinously thick parka would have cushioned the blow and I'm pretty sure I would have bounced off the floor like a beach ball.

After I regain my footing, I grab a hand basket and head straight to the refrigerated section, where I violate societal law by seizing the nearest carton of eggs without checking if any are cracked. I just want to get out of here as quickly as humanly possible, even if I have to deal with a broken egg or two after the fact.

I hastily toss a container of milk, imitation cheddar cheese sauce, tortilla chips, and blueberry muffins on top of the eggs without any regard for their safety. An older woman in a dark brown mink coat hovers near the butter display right in front of the last remaining package of Kerrygold on the refrigerated shelf. I grasp the gold-and-green box for dear life as the woman's ruby, knifelike claws dig into my hand.

"I was here first. That butter is mine," she squawks.

"If you were here first, then you would be holding it, wouldn't you?" I growl back.

We glare at each other, and she huffs about ten seconds into the faceoff, "Well, then." The woman selects a different brand of butter in defeat and rolls her cart away with a loud, "Tsk, tsk" resounding off the ceiling and indentations from her talons lingering in my palms.

Shannon would be immensely impressed with my instigating a dairy-aisle throw down for the coveted Irish gold. An instrumental version of a song she absolutely despises pipes through the store's speakers, and I chuckle at the irony it began to play the precise moment she crossed my mind. I make a mental note to telephone her later since she hasn't replied to my texts from last night.

Or any of my calls or texts since her —*Hey, you. Love you.*— message, either.

I sprint through the frozen food section on my way to check out and a quart of forbidden chocolate ice cream sings to me like a Siren from behind the glass display door. Without hesitation or shame, I snatch it up, along with a family-size frozen lasagna.

I know, it's negative zero degrees out, why the hell do I need ice cream?

Because I'm human.

And a lasagna big enough to feed a family of four?

Ditto.

I purposely pick the line at Checkout Four because I do not recognize the sour-faced cashier as a student or a graduate from school, which means I will not have to exchange the obligatory nicety-nice chitchat with her.

Sour Face sneers as she scans the ice cream. "Isn't it a little cold for this?"

I mirror her derisive smirk and retort through my teeth, "Listen, girlie, it doesn't matter whether it's stupid cold like today or hotter than hell, there will be days when ice cream is your only salvation, too." As our eyes connect, we recognize ourselves inside each other's bruised soul and our hardened faces soften.

My cell phone rings from inside my purse just as I take the handles of my grocery bags into my hands. I juggle everything like a circus clown and see Shannon's name flashing on the display. "Hey, Shan. I'm so happy it's you. Merry, merry and all that jazz…"

Oliver's voice interrupts me and blurts out, "Shannon passed away last night."

I stop dead in my tracks and stammer, "Wh…wh…what…did you just say?"

He repeats the godawful sentence through monstrous sobs. "I'm serious…Shannon…passed away…last night."

I drop to the ground and wail, "Oh, my God, Oliver, what happened?"

"I don't know…she woke up around two in the morning screaming about a headache…she convulsed and collapsed. I dialed 911…tried CPR…but…too late. Dammit, I tried…I tried so fucking hard to keep her alive."

"Shit, you've got to be kidding." I cough through my cries and pay no attention to the customers stepping to avoid my groceries, which have spilled all over and now ooze with gooey egg innards.

"Kel…" Oliver's voice quavers, "can you…meet me and Deirdre at Bolton's at two o'clock? We…I can't do this alone."

"I'll be there," I whisper.

I huddle in the corner of Food King's exit vestibule quivering for God knows how long, with my Kerrygold butter reduced to a heap of disgusting, slimy slop.

Part Three: The Future, or Rebirth

"Welcome, O life! I go to encounter for the millionth time the reality of experience and to forge in the smithy of my soul the uncreated conscience of my race."

James Joyce, *Ulysses*

Chapter One

I rummage through my backpack and locate the guidebook I shoved into it hours ago. "It's got to be around here someplace," I grumble while wrangling the book and my phone in my hands.

With the Dublin City Gallery Hugh Lane to my left and the Remembrance Garden behind me, the Dublin Writers Museum building blends into the scenery so well I have trouble pinpointing it through the mist. The cheerfully dismal morning is dreamlike, full of gray and wet, and I suspect the weather is outright mocking me while I attempt to find my bearings.

I grapple to slide my phone into my jacket's pocket, but it tumbles out of my hand and lands next to a puddle. A displeasing heat, hot as blazes, spreads across my face. "What the hell am I even doing here?" I mutter to myself. "I travel over an ocean on a whim, and for what?" I pick up my phone, wipe it dry on the bottom of my shirt, and push my hair out of my face, then groan loud enough to stir the nearby magpies who take flight without warning. A combination of exhaustion and frustration builds behind my skull and makes me feel like a fool.

There it is, dammit, right where it is supposed to be. The camouflaged Dublin Writers Museum, with its black iron fence and gilded letters, glowers at me in pious contempt.

I pan my sight to the left and do a double take as I spot something astonishing.

Chapter One.

The sign for the restaurant adjacent to the museum.

I casually gaze to my left and to my right expecting to find a hidden camera crew filming me, but I am alone, and nobody is watching me.

Nobody except the universe.

I stare at the sign.

My eyes aren't playing tricks on me, and my brain is not making me see something that does not exist.

It is there, right in front of me, an actual sign this time.

Chapter One.

I rip my copy of *Portrait* from my backpack and read Shannon's inscription—

Kelly,

You are a great teacher, but I see the writer behind your eyes. You don't know where to start? Start like Joyce did. Just sit down and write. Once you write chapter one, everything will fall into place. Don't deny your calling. "I mean, said Stephen, that I was not myself as I am now, as I had to become." James Joyce, Portrait. *Like Stephen, you are not yourself as you are now, as you have to become. This moment is everything. Follow the light and trust the journey as you move forward toward your true purpose.*

With gratitude and love,

Enduring the Waves

Your friend always,
Shannon

She referenced chapter one.

As I add this unmistakable and literal sign to the log of breadcrumbs from the universe I keep in my journal, a calming electricity travels through me. I take a picture of the sign and my inner voice reassures me.

"This is your first step. Now, trust everything will fall into place," I hear it speak.

"It's about time," I say out loud.

"About time for what?" asks a chestnut-haired man about my age, who is mid air leaping over a puddle. He lands solid without dropping his book or spilling his coffee. He has easy, hazel irises and a distinctive air of amiability.

"It's time for my chapter one," I timidly reply. "It's time to live."

"Slainte, love. Live on." He tips his tweed newsboy cap before heading in the direction of the River Liffey.

I stand tall and firm in Dublin, Ireland, on the north side of Parnell Square, and glimpse upward to the somber skies with a radiating grin and a single tear rolling down my cheek.

****

I wake from my nap and sit straight up with a start. My chest rapidly rises and falls from heavy breaths and a racing pulse, and the strange décor and furnishings further muddle my disorientation. "Where am I?" I blurt out, then I remember I'm in my room at Bloom's Hotel in Dublin.

My red-eye flight landed well before the hotel's check-in time, and my brief jaunt over to the Dublin Writers Museum helped pass the time. The hotel telephoned me on my cell at noon to inform me my room was ready, and as soon as I closed the door behind me, I crashed onto my bed and fell asleep almost instantaneously.

I stretch my muscles by elongating my arms and legs then wander over to the window. It's a mystery why my feet now stand in a room built upon Irish soil, but I have faith in the universe and believe it knows best. I trusted when it dealt Bloom's Hotel as the top card every single time I shuffled and searched the Internet for possible places to stay if I followed the countless signs collectively pointing to one location—Dublin, Ireland.

Bloom, as in Leopold Bloom, from *Ulysses*.

Shannon's favorite book.

The vibration from the traffic's hustle and bustle below massages my forehead, which I've pressed against the thick window pane.

I'm here.

I mean, I am really here, in Dublin.

My wristwatch still displays New Jersey time, but my cell phone displays the correct time for Dublin—4:30 in the afternoon. My stomach rumbles loud, reminding me it's been at least twelve hours since I choked down a measly croissant-and-yogurt boxed snack on the plane. I snatch a bag of pretzels from my carry on, and as I gobble down what's left in the package, I catch sight of my disheveled self in the mirror.

Geez-a-loo, what a haggard monster.

I clean myself up as fast as I can, pull my hair into a ponytail, and change into fresh clothes. Within minutes, I emerge from the hotel's front entrance into the Promised Land of Eire with a curious appetite for both sustenance and for life. I cross the street and find my room's window on the third floor and gasp.

A massive and vivid painted Stephen Dedalus lives on the exterior near it. Like my silhouetted self in the Smuggler's room, prior to punching her, of course, Dedalus is one of several Joycean characters featured in a vibrantly elaborate mural wrapping around the hotel's exterior.

How about that for validation I am in the right place at the right time?

After taking a few snapshots of the hotel, I amble two blocks over to the area surrounding Trinity College, which the author of my Dublin guidebook recommends as a must see. Double-decker buses and scores of people on bicycles zip past me in both directions.

I marvel at their collective expertise in driving the wrong way.

Hold on…

To them, it's the right direction, correct?

Correct.

The street scene fascinates me, but my hankering for food reminds me of one of my exploration's purposes. With no shortage of places to eat, I mosey along the labyrinth of streets made from stone and cobble surrounding the Trinity College campus. My curiosity transcends my hunger and I wander in wonder between pedestrians, bicycles, and the multitude of buses dropping off and picking up passengers. I recognize the melody of a song I haven't heard in ages flowing from an open doorway on the opposite side of Nassau Street, the lyrics telling a story about someone being a face in the crowd.

I snicker at a sign hanging above a storefront with a sign above its door reading "Knobs and Knockers" and pause to scribble both the song and the name of the store in my journal.

"Yo, lady, get da hell outta the way," a short, stocky man with a thick Brooklyn drawl bellows after stumbling into me.

I mumble a halfhearted apology and move to stand along the black rigid fence bordering the college grounds. I finish writing then shift my gaze upward to a tall, brick building with "Finn's Hotel" emblazoned upon its exterior in faded white stenciled letters. I vaguely recall Shannon once telling me she wanted a pair of Boston Terriers named Finn and Nora because James Joyce met his love, Nora Barnacle, at Finn's Hotel in Dublin.

Could it be?

I follow the sidewalk to the front of the building, and sure enough, my hunch is correct. Two painted announcements framing the doorway proclaim this is the exact spot where Joyce met his muse and future wife, Nora Barnacle, who worked as a chambermaid at the former hotel. In my mind's eye, I imagine the couple walking hand in hand along the same route I just traveled myself. I take a picture of my fortuitous discovery then eavesdrop on a conversation between two young gentlemen sitting on the curb.

"Wilde surely is a worthier writer than Beckett," one of them argues.

"Stop your poormouthing. Beckett is supreme talent. Wilde is a stook and a gobshite," the other fires back.

Both men cease talking and turn their heads toward me in unison. They gawk at me like I've got snakes growing from my scalp instead of hair. I whip around and head back in the direction I just came and giggle at the topic of their conversation. Shannon would have loved to hear those blokes squabbling over writers and literature instead of sports teams or whether a particular brand of beer tasted great or was less filling.

I forget traffic flows from the opposite direction and assume the coast is clear when there are no vehicles to my left, but I promptly step right in front of a taxicab. As the driver slams on his brakes just in the nick of time, I freeze like a deer in headlights. "Shite you, bloomin' tourist," he hollers over his blaring horn, and I bolt across to the sidewalk with equal parts of adrenaline and relief coursing through my veins.

My narrow escape leaves me breathless, and doubts strangle my mind like a psycho killer. I'm in a foreign country making an enormous ass out of myself, and for what reason? Flames radiate from my face just like in front of the museum and I smear my stinging tears away with the palms of my hands.

I allow the moment's humiliation to hold its own, then with more awareness, I rejoin life on Nassau Street. The vantage on this side of the road is quite different, with more locals in the crowd, students getting out of class, and people getting off from work versus the throngs of tourists who clogged the area just a short time ago.

I merge into the deluge surging toward Grafton Street like a fish swimming with its school, and tingles rush up and down my arms and legs. I feel a peculiar sense of familiarity, like I've been here before.

I suddenly spy shining, reddish hair about four people ahead of me, hair I recognize at once.

Identical tortoise-shell sunglasses hang off her nose,

and I draw in my breath as she turns her head to reveal the exact facial profile.

Holy crap, it *is* her.

I trail that red hair like a bloodhound. Shannon's doppelganger expertly threads between the vehicular traffic then weaves through the innumerable people on Grafton. I fall in step behind her and panic for a split second when I momentarily lose sight of her, but then the hair darts left onto Duke Street and into a place called Davy Byrnes.

I loiter outside the pub with the oddly familiar name.

Well, here goes nothing.

I casually stroll through the mostly empty pub like a detective looking for a missing person. My gaze scours the entire establishment, but I don't spot the mystery woman.

She's got to be in here, so I will wait it out.

After sitting on a stool where I can see almost every high-traffic area, the bartender asks with a fabulous Irish accent, "What'll it be, love?"

"What kind of soft drinks do you have?" I absently inquire while combing through my wallet for money.

"For minerals, I have cola, lemon lime, orange, and of course, beer and whiskey if you feel so inclined."

"Orange, please."

"As you wish." He fills a glass with ice and places it in front of me along with an open glass bottle. I hand him three euros, and when his hazel eyes meet mine, he slaps his palm against his forehead. "Go way outta that, weren't you over by Parnell Square earlier today?"

I am face to face with the chestnut-haired puddle jumper I encountered in front of the Dublin Writers Museum.

I blush and stammer, "Um...yes, that was me. I must have...um...looked like a moron...um...sorry."

"No need to apologize, and you're certainly no eejit." He extends his hand. "My name is Jame, and I didn't mean to rhyme in time. Jame Flaherty."

"It's a pleasure to meet you, Jame." I shake his hand with the redness dissipating from my cheeks. "I'm Kelly Lynch."

Three gentlemen clad in suits saddle up at the end of the bar. Jame winks at me and says, "Duty calls, but I'll be back." He attends the other customers, and after I take a satisfying drink, I start a new page of splendidly curious coincidences in my notebook—"Jame run-in twice, tender hazel eyes."

Since Shannon passed away six months ago, the universe has filled my life with signs leading me here, to Dublin. I'm talking about ten journal pages full of signs and counting. I have no doubt this man, who I have now spontaneously run into twice in a matter of hours in a city of over five hundred thousand people, is another breadcrumb because, just like all of the other signs, it is too mysteriously certain.

"Are you here on holiday or for business?" Jame's voice brings me round.

"I guess I'm here on holiday?"

"You guess?" When I furrow my brow, he adds, "Sorry, love. I didn't mean to make you feel like an amadan. That means awkward."

"No, it's okay. To be honest, I am not really sure why I'm here."

"Interesting response. Soon enough, I'm sure you'll figure out why. Are you traveling alone or with family or friends?"

"I'm by myself. My husband passed away in November, and it's just Dad and my brother for family."

"I'm sorry to hear about your loss. Been difficult, I'm sure."

His intrinsic tenderness urges me to continue. "Difficult is an understatement, and things went more downhill when my best friend died a month later."

"Shite, how terrible." A customer waves a ten euro note in the air and Jame bends toward me. "I'll return shortly."

The Irish whiskey bottles standing at attention behind the bar make me think of Shannon. I wish so badly she was sitting next to me just like all those times at Delancy's I took for granted. After the initial, tight camaraderie at school after her passing, a dark shroud hovered over everyone, and we mutually distanced ourselves from each other for reasons I cannot explain.

However, it was even more difficult for me. My double dose of grief repelled both my words and my connection to others, including my coworkers and students, and I felt more detached than ever from a job that used to mean everything to me.

When the signs pointing to Dublin started to surface from the great beyond, I made the mistake of telling Monica and Del about them. Monica thought I was crazy, and Del doubted with skepticism, saying traveling to Dublin on a whim would be foolhardy. "Leave the dead, dead," she said. "It's time to move on. Shannon wouldn't want you grasping at straws like this."

But I credit Shannon with dropping those straws for me, something neither of them could ever understand.

I alienated myself from everything school related, including the traditional Friday afternoon gatherings at

Delancy's, for the remainder of the school year. Just Dad and Christian know about my travel plans, and neither of them badgered me about my choice to follow the signs here, to Dublin.

I check my phone, but I have no missed calls or messages. I power it down and vow to keep it off for the duration of my trip. I mouth the words, "Be right back" to Jame as he fills a glass for another bar patron, and after he winks at me, something new and thrilling rushes through my veins. I head to the restroom a little too giddily, almost like one of my female students after her crush of the day says hello to her.

I tug the bathroom's entrance door handle toward me on my way out at the same time someone on the other side pushes it in.

The person and I almost collide, and as I take a step backward, our eyes meet.

I am staring straight into Shannon's shamrock eyes.

"Slainte," the woman says as she passes by me then closes and locks the stall door behind her.

Disbelief renders me motionless in the vestibule for a few seconds. I eventually make my way back to the bar, where I stumble when trying to climb back onto my barstool.

"Jaysus, are you all right?" Jame rushes over. "You look like you saw a ghost."

"I think I did," I faintly mumble.

"You're quivering like a frightened babby." He pours water into a glassful of ice and hands it to me. "Here, this will calm you."

A woman's voice commands from behind me, "Jame, a pint, stat."

"Aye, sis." Jame pulls down the beer tap, its golden

stream filling the glass in no time. He places it on the bar and says, "Siannon, allow me to introduce you to Kelly. She is visiting from…" He glances at me. "By your accent, I'd guess New Jersey?"

"Very good, Jame." I set down the glass of water with my trembling a bit subsided. "You know your accents."

Siannon holds out her hand to me but as I gasp, she swiftly recoils. "By your large eyes, I see I sicken you," she condemns in jest.

"No, I mean," I awkwardly falter, "I'm sorry. It's just…you are her double…your hair…your eyes…the shape of your face…"

"Stall the ball…Siannon's the ghost, no codding. I finally have something on my sis."

Hotness creeps up the back of my neck. "Please forgive me, I don't mean to offend you, but my God, you're the face in the crowd and could be my best friend's twin, Shannon, she passed away in December. The resemblance startled me."

"A fellow gingernut named Shannon? That's gone in the head. Do you have a photograph of your friend? While I'm sorry for your loss, I'd love to take a look at my double from the States."

I dig out a mangled photograph tucked away inside the pages of my copy of *Ulysses*. "This is one of the only pictures I have of us together—" I hand it to Siannon. "—taken at her wedding last November."

They both study the picture and Jame shudders. "Shite, sis, it is you."

"Apology accepted. You were not acting the maggot when you said she was my double." Siannon hands me back the photo, downs her pint, and slams her glass onto the bar in true Shannon-like fashion. "Bloody hell, Jame, I'm late. Nice to have made your acquaintance, Kelly." She scurries toward the entrance with her crimson scarf trailing behind her like a kite's tail.

"She's got a class at seven," Jame explains as he refills my water. "We're both studying at Trinity College. When Mam got sick, we quit going to university, but we swore to her on her death bed we'd finish someday, and we're making good on our promise."

"It took me a while to get my academic act together too, but for different reasons. My degree is in English, lots of literature there, and I teach British Literature at home."

"I knew we had something in common. Who is your favorite author?"

"I don't necessarily have a favorite author, but my favorite works to teach are 'Beowulf' and 'Macbeth.' "

"The question of the day, then, is this." He gesticulates for dramatic effect. "What do you think about James Joyce, Dublin's literary son?"

I breathe in deeply then let it out slowly. "Two years ago, I would have scoffed at the very idea of James Joyce. I hated him until Shannon schooled me. She forced me to read *Portrait* and *Ulysses*, and to my surprise, I regarded myself and everything else differently after reading both. To me, Joyce is Shannon, but she said to her, I was Dedalus. I guess that makes little sense." I shift my gaze to my hand resting on the bar rail.

"It makes perfect sense. I happen to know a little about Joyce, and while Shannon would be disappointed you missed Dublin's Bloomsday celebration by a measly three days, I bet she'd be overjoyed you are sitting in Davy Byrnes Moral Pub right now."

"You mean"—my eyes grow in size—"the one Leopold went to in *Ulysses*?"

"The one and only."

"The name sounded familiar, but I couldn't place it. You're right, Shannon would enjoy this." I gaze around the room to find just about every stool and seat occupied. "But I don't want to take you away from your responsibilities, Jame, and I'm starving, so maybe I should shove off."

"Nonsense. It's good craic having you here. Patsy's coming on soon, so I'll have a hand until my shift ends at ten. And if you're hungry, here's a menu to peruse—" He passes me a laminated card. "—I don't care for Leopold's choice of a gorgonzola sandwich. Beef stew and fish and chips are my two favorites."

"I'll take the fish and chips, and thank you, Jame. It's been a long time since I've had someone to talk to."

"My pleasure, love. Let me pull my socks up, and I'll check in with you in a little while." He flashes a smile then heads to the kitchen.

He wants me to stay.

It has to mean something, all of this. For certain, Shannon has led me right where the universe wants me to be.

****

"I am off the clock," Jame pronounces at one minute after ten. "I'd be honored to accompany you back to your hotel, Kelly."

"I'd enjoy that."

We exit Davy Byrnes and I can't help but whirl around in a circle while regarding the sky. "This is amazing. It's still light out and it's after ten. At home, the sun sets about eight thirty at this time of year, and it's mostly dark by nine or so."

"Little did I know when I woke up this morning, I'd be escorting a beautiful and spirited bird from the States back to her hotel this evening."

"Little did I know a week ago my feet would be walking on Dublin's streets right now." I skew my head and wonder. "Is this the middle of the city?"

"Your hotel is in the Temple Bar area, which is a popular area for tourists. The Grafton area here is known for its shopping and its street performers, or buskers. Many famous Irish musicians started their careers on this very street. Dublin's vicinities and quays mesh and meld with history and culture, but depending on the map you are viewing, yes, this might be the middle of the city."

"I just can't believe I'm here." I spread my arms out wide.

"Here, stay by me. I don't want you to encounter a chancer in this crowd."

"While it's still light, and on a weeknight?"

"Indeed." He takes my hand, his touch making my stomach flutter, and leads me along the uneven cobblestone through the street performers and revelers.

He gestures with his head toward a life-size bronze busty woman with a basket-filled cart on our right. "There she is, Molly Malone. She's one of Dublin's most prominent landmarks. Legend has it Molly was a fishmonger by day, and a bed monger by night, so to speak." He raises his eyebrow. "You know, a doxie, or as you might say, a prostitute."

"I guess she did what she had to do."

"Did you ever hear the song about her?"

"It doesn't ring a bell."

Jame sings loudly in deep baritone, "She was a fishmonger, And sure, 'twas no wonder, For so were her mother and father before, And they wheeled their barrow, Through the streets broad and narrow, Crying 'cockles and mussels, alive, alive, oh. Alive, alive, oh alive, alive, oh,' crying 'cockles and mussels, alive, alive, oh.' "

A few Dubliners join his performance without skipping a beat. They bellow in unison, "She died of a fever, And sure, no one could save her, And that was the end of sweet Molly Malone, Now her ghost wheels her barrow, Through the streets broad and narrow, Crying 'cockles and mussels, alive, alive, oh. Alive, alive, oh, Alive, alive, oh,' Crying 'cockles and mussels, alive, alive, oh.' "

The forming crowd bursts into applause, and as Jame peels away toward me, I exclaim, "I usually shy away from impromptu performances in fear of being forced to participate, but that was absolutely fabulous."

"All in a Dublin's day, my dear." A slight twinkle shimmers in his eyes and I sense my cheekbones becoming more defined by my elongated grin. I try to conceal my gaiety by yawning, but Jame teases me. "So I go all out to impress this teacher from New Jersey, and she's bleedin' knackered."

I laugh at his playful contempt. "Your performance was magnificent, but I've done more in the last forty-eight hours than I think I've done in the past two years. The activity, combined with the jetlag, is catching up with me a bit."

He laces his fingers with mine. "Just gassing. It's grand being with you."

"I can't remember when I've had this much fun. Back in my heyday, I thought I had to be liquored up to have a good time, but I despised the hazy recollections of whatever I did the night before and associated morning-after guilt. One of the many reasons I chose to give up drinking."

"I understand more than you know." Jame shifts his gaze upwards. "I always loved the pub. It was lively and loud, and I belonged there. After Mam died, the pints were my crutch, and I was ossified to hell every waking moment. I lied to myself, and to everyone around me, about the gargle relieving my grief. Truth is, I heard Mam every day crooning in my head, 'Jamey, now, get a hold of yourself. You're better than this polluted fecker you've become.' So I got off the drink, but I kept the pub." He shoots me a timid smile. "You must be thinking, 'What a wanker this guy is, he won't shut his cake hole.' "

"Not at all."

"What are your plans while you're in Dublin, Kelly?"

I shrugged my shoulders. "I came here on such a whim I figured I'd wing it and look upon what Shannon would have wanted to see before I fly home on Tuesday. She was Irish and loved James Joyce, and it was her lifelong dream to come to Dublin and see with her own eyes what she read about. She never got the chance, so my mission is to see the Joycean sights through her eyes with mine."

Jame slows his pace as we approach Bloom's Hotel. "And I bet you aren't sure where to start."

"Exactly, and it's a little intimidating. How did you know?"

"Just a hunch."

We wander into the empty lobby, and he gestures to the end of the check-in counter. "I'll be waiting right there tomorrow morning at ten if you'd like a personal tour guide."

"Are you sure, Jame? You've got to have other things you should be doing…studying, laundry, family, errands."

"Aye, I'm free all day, and it would be my pleasure to squire you around our fine city."

"Okay, then, I'm in"—I nod likewise—"and I'll meet you there at ten."

He bows and chivalrously kisses my hand. "Until tomorrow, love."

"Until tomorrow."

I float down the hallway to the lift, my face beaming and my being aquiver, unaware Jame lingers in the lobby until the lift's doors close.

****

When the same doors glide open the next morning, I scurry to the lobby and pay no mind to how absurd my face must appear when I spy Jame leaning against the counter where he vowed he would be. "I tried to beat you by ten minutes, but here you are, a man of your word, and early to boot."

"It's not every day I can reveal my mental vat of useless knowledge on an American lass. Ready for our exploration?"

"I sure am."

He holds the door open for me and nods to the sky. "The sun came out for you, love, which doesn't happen every day here in Dublin. Today we will pay a visit to several places I believe your friend would have wanted to see."

As I take my first steps along today's escapade, I wistfully search the heavens above me and think to myself, "This is for you, Shannon."

Jame's voice centers me in the present moment. "It's fascinating, Kelly, the things right in front of us we miss or outright ignore. There's so much, literally steps away from your hotel, yet most never pay attention to those details or the lessons we can learn from them." Both his voice and his pace hesitates. "If any good came from Mam's death, I now understand the value of life and I revere every moment, whether it is good, or bad, or even if I don't know what in Jaysus is going on."

"I agree with you. The last year surely taught me life is precious."

"You are bang on." He opens his arms wide. "This area here, which we also walked through last night, is known as College Green. We will head through the Green, go past the bank, then travel down Westmoreland."

"Is the old building, with the pillars and the figures near the top, the bank?"

He stops in front of its steps. "Yes, I am quite certain it has been a bank ever since the early 1800s. This is the same bank where Stephen Dedalus cashed the prizes he won at Belvedere College so he could buy those expensive presents for his family in *Portrait*."

"Impressive you know that off the top of your head."

"As long as a pigeon doesn't poo on top of my head." Jame chuckles, but I miss his point. "Another allusion to Joyce, the pigeon comment is from *Ulysses*. Mam began reading Joyce to me when I was a youngster." He nods his head in the direction of a sculpture on a triangle island across the street from us. "We are headed there."

Car after bus after truck speeds between us and our destination and I cry out, "We'll never make it there with all of this traffic."

He clasps my hand with his and yells, "Run fast but mind yourself!" We zip across the intersection, and when our feet safely land on the island's curb, we giggle from the adrenaline.

After I catch my breath, I say, "I guess I can trust you because if you wanted to do me harm, you would have shoved me in front of those buses. Is that a statue of Joyce? I didn't know he wore a cape."

"No, this is Thomas Moore. He graduated from Trinity College in the year 1799 and wrote volumes of poetry and songs."

"His name doesn't ring a bell. Should it?"

"If you've read *Ulysses*, you've heard of him." He shifts and points toward the ground in front of Moore's likeness. "Come and read this."

"Okay." Jame's directive intrigues me, and I stride over to discover a worn rectangular bronze plaque with an intricate engraving inlaid in the concrete. I read the inscription aloud, "He crossed under Tommy Moore's roguish finger. They did right to put him up over a urinal; meeting of the waters." I gaze up and scratch my temple. "Hmmm…I have no idea."

"Look closer. Does the marker provide you with any other clues?"

"Let me see—" I bend down to inspect it. "—no, it's just a…wait a minute. There's a man wearing glasses, a suit, and a round, brimmed hat. And there, it says *Ulysses*." I glance up at Jame's sly grin. "I read *Ulysses* last summer, although Shannon could recite much of it from memory. I am guessing the quote is from the book? The man with the round hat, is he supposed to be Stephen?"

"You are correct, the quote is from *Ulysses*, like my earlier pigeon quip, but Stephen he is not. It's our main character, good old Leopold. There are several other markers scattered about Dublin memorializing locations along Bloom's walking route."

"Did Bloom really pass by this exact spot?" I ponder and snap a picture of the plaque with my camera.

"Yes, he did. Joyce is referring to Moore's poem titled 'The Meeting of the Waters.' There"—he gestures his head to the left—"the site of the first public toilets in Dublin. When Bloom passes by them, he acknowledges the placement of the Moore memorial near the toilets, no doubt, a crass Joycean take on a different type of 'meeting of the waters,' so to speak. In his poem, however, Moore wrote about the intersection of two rivers in county Wicklow. They combine into the Avoca then flow into the Irish sea near the town of Arklow, which in Irish means 'the big inlet…' "

I jerk my head in his direction. "Did you say inlet?"

"Ahhh, your sparkling wide eyes tell me I've stumbled upon something dear to you," Jame exclaims then removes a worn book from his rucksack. He pages through the volume then reads aloud as I listen intently, my face toward the sky as Jame's bass strings sound the words—

"There is not in the wide world a valley so sweet
As that vale in whose bosom the bright waters meet;
Oh! the last rays of feeling and life must depart,
Ere the bloom of that valley shall fade from my

heart.

Yet it was not that nature had shed o'er the scene
Her purest of crystal and brightest of green;
'Twas not her soft magic of streamlet or hill,
Oh! no—it was something more exquisite still.
'Twas that friends, the beloved of my bosom, were near,
Who made every dear scene of enchantment more dear,
And who felt how the best charms of nature improve,
When we see them reflected from looks that we love.
Sweet vale of Avoca! how calm could I rest
In thy bosom of shade, with the friends I love best,
Where the storms that we feel in this cold world should cease,
And our hearts, like thy waters, be mingled in peace."

I rub the corner of my eye with my pinky. "May I please see your book?"

"Of course." He hands it to me, still open to Moore's poem.

I read again in silence "The Meeting of the Waters," then utter, "Shannon, she's the friend. The storm in my heart is the grief from losing both her and Wayne." I gesture toward the sky. "Shannon definitely made life better, or as Moore puts it, more dear, and Wayne did too, once upon a time ago."

"Life can still be dear." He wraps his arm around me. "Here's a seemingly unimportant part of Bloom's day when he strides past the statue of Thomas Moore and makes a vulgar bathroom joke. The greater meaning, the greater understanding is the message you interpret in Moore's poem, but how many of us pause to take in the entirety of a moment like you just did? Most of us go about our days without paying attention to the magnitude of the present, which is truly a miracle no matter how inconsequential or mundane it might appear."

"All of that from an accidentally deliberate quote, undoubtedly another sign from the great beyond."

"Let me take your picture with the roguish Tommy Moore to memorialize the exact minute you enriched your life by following in the footsteps of Bloom, Dedalus, and Joyce himself, amongst so many others."

He clicks the shutter button a few times, and I can't help myself from flinging my arms around him when he hands my camera back to me.

His voice susurrates in my left ear, "Your friend is here, in you. You have taken your first steps into a new awareness, and we have only traveled three blocks. Just imagine what is waiting for us up ahead." We separate and he points to the crook of his arm. "Ready to continue your mission from the universe?"

With tingling chills trickling over my extremities, I thread my arm through his. "Definitely. Let's do this."

****

Jame's expertly prepared walking tour guides me to several additional bronze *Ulysses* markers and other places found within the book's pages, including a Chinese restaurant on Westmoreland Street called Harrison's in Bloom's time. Jame jokes we won't be able to order mock-turtle soup or jam puffs there like Leopold. "But I hear they serve a delicious Peking duck," he jibes. We stroll past the National Library, where Bloom darted in to avoid his wife's lover, and the site on Dawson Street where Bloom aided a blind man with crossing the road.

At Sweny's Pharmacy, I buy lemon soap just like Leopold Bloom did. Jame even sings along with the "pharmacist" on duty, who in reality is a volunteer actor-musician who performs for tourists like me who visit Sweny's for the same reason.

Lemon soap is Sweny's top seller and smells divine.

We take a short detour to honor another Irish literary giant, Oscar Wilde, and I pose alongside his likeness in Merrion Square before we pass Finn's Hotel, then lounge on Trinity College's flawlessly landscaped courtyard.

After taking a sip of water, I nod toward the entry gate. "Out there, after I spotted Finn's on my own yesterday, that's where I thought I saw Shannon, but she ended up being your sister. I just had to follow her, and I'm glad I did because she led me straight to Davy Byrnes and to you."

Jame wipes his forehead with his handkerchief and inquires, "Tell me, love, what happened to Shannon?"

"It was so unexpected. She stayed with me almost every waking minute the week after Wayne was killed but fell into a terrible depression after losing her baby. A few weeks later, she suffered an aneurysm in her sleep and was gone."

I yank up the bottom of my jeans to show Jame the purple butterfly tattoo on my right ankle. "She got a tattoo like this to symbolize her transformation when she decided to earn her master's degree. The program was supposed to make her lifelong dream of studying here in Dublin come true, but she died before she had the chance."

I will back the waterworks building behind my misty eyes, gather myself, and continue, "Sorry, sometimes it still gets to me. The foggy funk that followed strangled my words and made my seclusion even worse, but also made me keenly aware of the signs leading me here to Dublin."

"What kind of signs?"

"Flyers for Ireland vacations I didn't request in my mailbox every day for a week, random Joyce quotes all of a sudden popping up everywhere, including a handwritten one on an index card which fell out of a used book about surfing I bought online, even an allusion to Chapter One, the restaurant over by the writer's museum in something Shannon wrote to me. The universe used those hints to lead me here, to this exact location where we are sitting right now."

"You are utterly savage for putting your faith in the cosmos and traveling here to Dublin to honor her. May I ask what happened to your husband?"

"He deliberately ran into traffic when he was drunk. Our marriage had its faults, but I never expected him to lose it like he did." I pick a blade of grass and weave it between my fingers. "My life has been one disaster after another. Drinking too much, flunking out of college, a spontaneous marriage, my job as a teacher, my stories, and journals…every single one a fruitless attempt to avoid my abusive mother or my drunk husband or my own imperfections or my empty life. But you know what? This moment, here…" I pat the grass.

"What, love?"

I shift my gaze in his direction, my hands solid on the ground. "Some might say impulsively running off to Dublin was also an escape." I pat the ground again. "But this moment might be the first time in my life when I've experienced absolute freedom. There are no demands from others, no itineraries or expectations from someone else I am forced to abide by, no shame or judgment. I'm free to be me and to participate in my life for once, rather than run away from it."

"Go on," he urges.

"The light. I've always believed it's shining ahead, but I've never been able to catch up to it. But sitting here with you…Shannon believed she'd find the missing part of her soul in Dublin, and my intuition tells me the universe is leading me to the light I've been searching for."

After a moment of quiet, Jame replies, "The most profound human experience is loss. The more we feel, even in our darkest times when we are just sick with sorrow, the more we are alive. Your life has finally begun. I may have only met you yesterday, but your strength, it's impressive."

I close my eyes and shake my head.

He continues, "Yes, for you have endured and prevailed. You're sitting in Dublin, for shite's sake, ready to take on the world, and from what I gather, it's very unlike you to do something, anything impulsive like this—" He covers my tear-filled eyes with his hands. "—and it is time for you to 'shut your eyes and see.' The light you are seeking? You will find it because it is shining ahead. In fact, it is shining right in front of you. All you have to do is acknowledge it."

I almost suffocate on my words and sniffle, "I think I see a tiny flickering."

The moment holds its own then dissolves into the past as a rumbling from my stomach pierces the silence and elicits a loud chuckle from both of us. "My apologies." I giggle and rub my eye sockets with my hands. "I've got a very noisy hunger alarm."

"I'm famished, too. Let's get something to eat." We rise to our feet and Jame links his fingers with mine then leads the way out of Trinity's iron gate. He shows me two more waypoints along Leopold Bloom's route on Grafton Street, one in front of the Bank of Ireland, and the other outside the swanky Marks and Spencer department store. "We are passing through one of the most expensive shopping areas in the world, even before Joyce's time. We were on this street last night."

"It feels rather different at this time of day."

"I want you to examine Davy's one more time through both Shannon's eyes and your new ones."

We halt in front of the pub, and he pronounces, "You are already aware Leopold Bloom ate lunch here at Davy Byrnes. What's by your feet?"

I find another Leopold-tracking plaque with the inscription, "He entered Davy Byrne's Moral Pub. He doesn't chat."

"Wow, I walked over this twice yesterday without noticing it, didn't I?" I shook my head.

"Yes, you did."

"You were correct when you said most people fail to find life's Easter eggs, but I'm learning."

"I'm glad you chatted, unlike Bloom. But Davy's pub is more than Leopold and Joyce. It was a favorite of Irish authors Brendan Behan, Patrick Kavanagh, Liam O'Flaherty, and James Stevens, and it also played a role in the 1916 revolution. Now, spin around."

"Spin around, like this?" I literally twirl in a circle like a child with my arms outstretched.

"I meant turn around, silly." He snickers and puts his hands on top of my shoulders and directs me in an about face. "The bar there, The Bailey, is also in *Ulysses*, except in Joyce's time, it was called 'The Burton.' Notice anything?"

I study the striped, canopied awnings and the patrons enjoying their lunch on the outside patio then call out, "There it is." I scamper over to another landmark. "His heart astir, he pushed in the door of the Burton restaurant," I read aloud.

My heart is also astir like Bloom's, but I keep that fact to myself.

"Another key spot for Irish literati including Beckett, Behan, and others. This is where Bloom was disgusted by how the other patrons were eating, hence why he ended up at Davy's. Either place is a fine location to relax with a good book and enjoy a bite or a pint."

"Are we going to eat here?"

"No, I don't want you to be disgusted like Bloom. We're heading back to Grafton."

A short stroll leads us to a building featuring a mosaic of ornate flowers made from small, square tiles outlining its frontage with red letters proclaiming its name "Bewley's Oriental Café" and a balcony suspended above the name. "If you don't mind tea and pastries for lunch, Bewley's is a must."

"I may have a lot to learn, Jame, but who am I to say no to pastries?"

" 'Dublin, I have much, much to learn.' Stephen said that, Dedalus—"

The host interrupts him. "May I help you?"

"Two, please, and we'll wait for the balcony."

"Yes, sir. Shan't be long," the host replies.

Jame's eyes meet mine, and I almost get lost in them. He repeats, " 'Dublin, my love. You have much, much to learn.' Just like Stephen."

"Shannon told me I reminded her of Stephen because I am both a teacher and a writer."

The host gestures for us to follow him upstairs, and as he directs us onto the narrow balcony framed by a red wrought-iron railing, he assures, "You'll have the whole balcony to yourself until another customer queries to sit here."

Despite the tight space, Jame manages to pull my chair out for me. Below us, Grafton Street bustles with tourists and shoppers, some of whom listen to a young, shock-haired gentleman strumming a guitar while crooning a disaffected grunge music ballad found at the top of the charts for a few weeks in the mid-nineties.

"As a bona fide local and a fellow Joycean," he says, "can I recommend a spot of tea and the Bewley's Mary Cake?"

"One of today's specials is strawberry shortcake with real cream and meringue, and strawberry shortcake is one of my favorites."

"As you wish."

After the server takes our orders, Jame pats the iron railing the same color as dull holly berries. "The unofficial term for this balcony is the James Joyce balcony because many believe Joyce frequented this spot on many occasions, and when he wrote the phrase 'the lofty clattery café' he was alluding to this very location."

My eyes widen. "Did he actually sit here, on this balcony, and write?"

"While nobody knows with absolute certainty, I like to think he did."

The server sets our tea and treats on the table, and I promptly salivate at the sight of my massive strawberry shortcake. I take one bite and sink into my seat. With my mouth full, I say, "Sorry for being a savage, but this is simply decadent. The pastry is light and flaky, the strawberries are bursting and ripe, and the cream, it's the best whipped cream I've ever tasted."

"Irish grass-fed cows make all the difference when it comes to dairy as opposed to those inferior American cows you're used to. How do you like your tea?"

"Sweet with lemon." My voice muffled by the pastry filling my mouth.

We drink our tea and eat dessert for lunch while life passes by below us, saying little yet smiling much. I sample a bite of Jame's Mary Cake and proclaim it the second-best cake I ever ate, the first being the strawberry shortcake I just destroyed.

When nothing but whipped cream residue remains on my plate, he asks, "So you mentioned earlier you are a writer. I've gotten to know Kelly the person and a bit about Kelly the teacher. Tell me about Kelly the writer."

I shift my gaze away and mutter, "I'm not sure Kelly the writer still exists."

"Pardon?"

"For real, I don't think Kelly the writer is alive anymore." I play with the crumbs on the table, my index finger becoming a plow of sorts as I work them into a tiny pile while I ignore my quivering lip.

"Kelly the writer is not dead. She's just been hibernating, waiting for a very lengthy winter to end. Tell me about her, and maybe we can figure out how to awaken her."

I smash the crumb pile I created with my palm. "I loved to write, and I thought I was good at it, but in reality, I was just another hack who wasted too many hours of her life writing up at the inlet."

"Aha." Jame's face lights up. "I've been waiting for the inlet to resurface since we stood in front of the Thomas Moore sculpture."

"The inlet was my happy place, and my favorite place to write, before my desire to write was decimated."

"What happened?"

"To be honest, I'd rather not get into the decade-old dreadful saga right now. I can deny it until the Irish dairy cows come home, but the truth is this—my soul's secret is, and always has been, I want to paint with words, but my palette is dry and my brushes barren. The more I try to force them out, the deeper they bury themselves. I just don't know anymore."

"You said earlier you've been escaping your whole life, and I doubt very much you are a hack." He tenderly caresses the top of my hand with his index finger. "Maybe your words are crippled because writing is no longer an escape but your purpose, your passion, your gift."

"I don't have any gifts."

"Yes, you do"—he nods—"for starters, you clearly are a good friend and have one hell of a sense of moxie, I think you call it? Change can be scary, especially taking a chance on the unknown, but for Jaysus sake, you took a chance and now you're sitting in Dublin. The more we fight against our destiny, the more complicated life becomes. Think about it. Rather than escaping or ignoring, submit to what is, right now, here. This moment is all we've got, and it's as real as real gets. Those words, they'll come in time. By leaving the past and accepting the present, the possibilities of what can be come alive."

I shiver despite the warm sun beating down upon us.

"Are you okay?" he asks.

A smile tugs on the corners of my mouth. "Yes, Jame. For once in my life, I think I am actually okay."

He holds me in his arms so tight I have difficulty breathing.

"I don't know what to say," I murmur into his ear.

"You don't have to say anything, love. Just be."

Chapter Two

I arise with the sun.
Yesterday's colorful memories and epiphanies vibrantly prance in my head and make my pulse quiver.
I don't hope.
Rather, I know I am where I belong.
No more regret.
No more cursing the words eluding me so.
No more second guessing myself.
Reminiscing about Jame's fingers intertwined with mine makes me giggle with girlish delight.
I throw the sheets off with abandon and stretch my legs, which ache from so much walking. After Bewley's on Grafton, Jame escorted me to the over eight hundred--year-old Dublin Castle via Dame Street. We wandered along the River Liffey and traversed both the Ha'Penny Bridge and the James Joyce Bridge, then we followed the labyrinth of alleys to the Temple Bar area with a visit to the renowned Temple Bar itself. We arrived back at Bloom's Hotel a little after one in the morning.
The butterflies in my stomach soar triple time as I ruminate about his goodbye kiss, which set both my legs and torso aflame. Our libidos lusted to do otherwise, but we agreed ending our day in the lobby was in both of our best interests. "We don't want to complicate things," he had said, and while my baser instincts craved to cross that proverbial line, I wisely concurred.

My tingling extremities, however, suggest I should have considered the alternative.

Jame has to work a double shift at Davy's and finish a paper he has to hand in on Tuesday, but he assured me we'd meet up tomorrow. He suggested a few nearby landmarks to discover on my own and provided me with information about each. "Go early because it's a Saturday and the streets will get crowded fast," he advised.

I heave open the drapes and the dismal, gray clouds welcome me.

Perfect Dublin weather.

I should get a move on.

After I shower and dress, I clasp Shannon's triskele necklace, which Deirdre gave me, around my neck.

I hope I'm making her proud.

With my umbrella, my journal, and my camera safely stored in my backpack, I head to the lift with an eager hope Jame might have been joshing me about his busy day. A fleeting pang of disappointment flows through me when the doors open to a deserted lobby but dissipates quickly as I reaffirm today is for me.

It doesn't take me long to cross over the River Liffey via the O'Connell Bridge, and I pause every few feet to note what I observe and hear: the vintage three-masted tall ship moored alongside the river's wall to my right, the raspy chatter from the black-and-white magpies, the tall cylindrical silver point screaming high in the sky from somewhere in front of me. My descriptions burst with color on my journal's page in spite of my monochrome surroundings.

I find the *Ulysses* plaque on Bachelor's Walk Jame told me about and snap a photograph of my feet framing it. *"As he set foot on the O'Connell Bridge a puffball smoke plumed up from the parapet,"* I read to myself. Jame's scribbling tells me the smoke in *Ulysses* came from a passing brewery barge.

An ornate and tarnished statue of a man standing atop three marble-like layers towers in front of me, with a seagull on his head and other petrified figures interposed below his feet. I learn from the inscription the man's name is Daniel O'Connell. "O'Connell Bridge, O'Connell Monument, and O'Connell Street," I wonder aloud.

"He wanted us Catholics to be allowed to vote, O'Connell, I mean."

Goosebumps scurry down my spine as the hot words ricochet off the back of my neck. I whip around to find an elderly woman with silver hair dressed all in black almost on top of me. "I didn't mean to startle you, dear," she says with a quintessential Irish accent.

"No worries." The woman exudes both a feeling of familiarity and an aura of brilliancy, so much so every one of my hairs stands on end with warm coolness.

"Oh, an American girl. Are you here on holiday or to study?"

"Originally just to visit, but now I speculate it's both."

Her soft, wrinkled hands clasp mine, and she muses, "Never stop learning, dear. This moment is everything."

I draw in my breath as I remember Jame saying those exact words yesterday. "What did you just say?"

"Only two things truly matter in life. One is this moment, which is absolutely extraordinary, but my instincts assure me you've recently learned this. The other thing that genuinely matters is you, if to nobody

...lf and to the universe. Your life will ...he moment you acknowledge your ...orth."

...voman's shamrock-green irises stir an unusu... ...plifting warmth in my soul. Her hands release mine, then she unsteadily wanders into the crowd and disappears.

I step aside to jot about the mysterious elder in my journal, then I recommence my exploration along O'Connell Street and stumble upon another *Ulysses* marker proclaiming the location to be the home of the Evening Telegraph, one of Dublin's daily newspapers during Bloom's time. The current inhabitant of the former newsroom's window displays entices me, and I wander wide-eyed into Easons. All my favorite things are under one roof…books, school supplies, souvenirs and curiosities, and even a café. I grab a latte and browse the nirvana like a kid in a candy store. I could have bought everything but settle upon three notebooks, a magnetic bookmark, and a limited-edition paperback copy of Joyce's *Dubliners*.

Jame's notes refer to a streetside statue of Joyce somewhere in the vicinity. "You can't miss The Spire, it's near there." He noted the 1916 Easter Rising skirmishes and some Irish Republican Army bombings occurred in this area of Dublin.

The tall point I spotted while walking over the O'Connell Bridge is The Spire. Like Jame said, it is impossible to miss because it looks like a giant unicorn horn projecting straight into the sky. I stand next to its base and peer up its shiny, soaring height which appears to connect to the heavens. In order to fit the Spire's massive altitude into my camera's view finder, I backstep across O'Connell Street onto an intersecting side street and click the shutter button. A group of non-English speakers clammer behind me on my right, and I pan my head toward them then gasp.

It's him.

Their tour leader snaps a group photo with him then holds her red pennant flag over her head, and the cluster follows her down the street like lemmings.

I inquisitively advance upon the bronzed James Joyce and see him with not only my own eyes, but with Shannon's as well. My anticipation increases with each forward stride, and I am completely and utterly aware.

Joyce pompously stares toward the sky, his signature cane in his right hand and a book in his left. He is veiled by an aura of palpable preeminence despite being inanimate.

Dauntlessness replaces my inferiority, and I say aloud to him, "So, sir, we finally meet."

I swear I hear the susurration of his voice within the wind, "Well, now you met me. What's next?"

"I don't know."

Two adolescent girls pass by and giggle at me having a conversation with a frigging statue. One mocks, "What a plonker."

I disregard them and run the tips of my fingers over the rough fold of his debonair jacket and the details in his tie, his face, his glasses, his crossed feet.

"Why me?" he interrogates. "I am just the prick with the stick, you know."

"Because Shannon never got to meet you. She never got to touch your jacket or sense the weight of your omniscient gaze. Because she told me I'm the everyman in your characters. I am also a writer."

"A writer you say?" he scoffs. "You have to write to be a writer. 'A man of genius makes no mistakes.' "

I audibly recite from memory the rest of his quote, "His errors are volitional and are the portals of discovery."

"So then, write. Write and discover yourself, girl."

Everyone else going about their business ignores the literary wizard standing on the same street, and I think, "Oh, Shannon. How I wish you were here with me. The prick with the stick, you'd just love this."

I hear the wind hum, "I am here."

I scan his wholeness one last time with both sets of eyes, then I acknowledge after clasping his rigid hand, "Thank you for inspiring me through my best friend."

While the real Joyce wouldn't give a damn about my gratitude, I swear Joyce the statue winks at me through his semblance of eminence.

His wink dictates my next location, which is a short distance away.

The James Joyce Centre.

As I roam along O'Connell Street to my destination, my surroundings enchant my senses: the songs of the bright red tourist hop-on hop-off bus engines, and the bongo-drum beaters wearing bohemian garb made from hemp, the savory fragrances escaping from the eateries, the texture of the General Post Office's ridged pillars, and the sandstone base of the vast monument memorializing Charles Stewart Parnell.

I hook a left then a right onto North Great George's Street.

Every front door along the street is brightly painted and representative of Dublin's traditional and charming Gregorian style, with almost every color of the rainbow represented. I think about the postcards on display at Easons and try to emulate the compositions with my camera. I shoot about twenty images of my favorite, the soothing, indigo door next to the sunny, yellow one, then I stand at attention in front of building number thirty-five.

The magnificent magnitude of what is in front of me reflects in my pulse. I ascend the brick stairs one at a time and open the navy-blue Gregorian door to enter The James Joyce Centre. The gentleman on duty at the counter takes my admission fee and suggests, "I recommend starting on the top floor and working your way down. And please remember to sign our guest register. Failte."

As I write my name in the guest book, I glance at the names above mine. Three visitors yesterday were also from New Jersey, Glenharbor to be specific.

Small world, for certain.

On my way toward the staircase, I study the detailed Joyce timeline painted on the wall and examine every photograph's caption while climbing the stairs like I am going to take an exam at the end of my visit.

The top floor is a maze of exhibits with various quotes from Joyce's works painted in white on the teal walls, and another curious sense of familiarity encompasses me. I read every word as I pass through the displays of period furniture and Joycean artifacts intermixed with modern multimedia presentations, and once again, I feel like I've been here before.

I peek into a modest room titled "The Writer at Work" and stand in awe at how cramped it is. The room is just large enough for a bed, a bookcase, and a petite bureau with clothes, books, photographs, and other items from Joyce's era strewn about, and its silence speaks to me.

These are the conditions Joyce wrote in every day.

Remorse for allowing my own life circumstances to shunt my writing takes me hostage. If Joyce wrote in such confined quarters, I have no right to allow writer's block or any other bullshit excuse to clog the flow of my words. I delicately brush the framed black-and-white portrait of Joyce on the bureau with my fingertips and sneeze from the small trail of dust that escapes into the air.

I pledge I will never again let my own physical or mental environment interfere with my writing.

Joyce wrote in chaos, and so will I.

I am renewed.

I meander down to the floor below Joyce's makeshift bedroom into an elegant, pastel-hued room filled with portraits of Joyce's family members on the walls and take a seat on a tall-back chair. Other guests sporadically enter and exit the room, but I pay them no attention.

I do not write.

I do not take any pictures.

At times, I do not even think.

I just sit still in the room and exist.

Without warning, various scenes from my life flash through my mind like a highlight reel: Wayne's sea glass blues, that putrid pink prom dress, cowering from my mother's fist and insults, Shannon's voice resounding her trademark phrase "Hey you," Thanksgiving with Dad, creating futuristic cities out of building blocks with Christian on his bedroom floor, sitting at Smuggler's and the sound of the pills hitting the current, the characters I gave life to on the pages of my notebooks, my college degree and my gradebook, the tears, the joy, the heartache, the self deprecation, the empty bottle after bottle after bottle I consumed, all of my various attempts at escaping reality, this one, treasured life I've been granted…

Every moment from my past led me to this moment, to sitting in this chair in the middle of The James Joyce Centre in Dublin, to the here and now.

My clarity is infinite and drips with my experiences, Shannon's legacy, and Joyce's influence.

I sit, speechless and numb, with an electric awareness of my true purpose engulfing every molecule of my existence with cold, clammy sparks.

This.

This moment.

It's everything.

I will run no more.

I will live, dammit, while I write the stories burning in my soul.

I am revitalized.

****

I reenter my hotel room delighted and drenched from the typical Dublin rain which christened me anew. Everything is wet: my hair, my feet, my clothes, everything except my spirit and my purchases, which remain protected inside the plastic center of my backpack along with my journal, camera, and wallet. I change into dry clothes then rip the plastic covering from the pristine, yellow notebook I bought at Easons.

I grasp a pencil I find hiding inside the room's desk drawer, sit upright on the bed, and open the notebook to the first sheet of lined paper. The pencil's sharpened tip rests there, on top of the pristine page, but I fight to produce the first word.

Come out, dammit.

The lead tip remains in the same position.

I refuse to give up.

I coerce the words out of my mind and onto the notebook's leaves.

A warm intensity suddenly flows from the top of my head through my shoulder then down my right arm and hand. The tip of my pencil bounces on the page and leaves a slanted lead line.

I

Another jolt produces the word "can," which is followed by "write."

I can write.

A ravenous vigor courses through my veins and triggers my pencil into furious motion. I am unaware of what I write as the frenzied words appear on the pages I violently flip after filling.

My pencil soon dulls, so I seize a black pen from my backpack and continue writing as ferociously as ever. I lose all track of time as words buried inside my soul for an eternity see the light of day. I misspell some words and compose incomplete sentences, but grammar and mechanics are of zero importance. I scribble with escalating intensity. My emotions shift by the second and run the gamut from elation to livid to delirious to sullen. Words about Wayne and Shannon and The Benevolenters and my loathsome mother and Jame and Joyce morph into the other's world with no regard for continuity.

The floodgates are open, and my words are a storm surge.

After I fill the last of the 250 pages in the yellow notebook, some pages with one word and others with four or more paragraphs, I claw the plastic from the second notebook, a purple one, and write, "I'm done apologizing for being human." I continue writing through teardrops and laughter, anger and joy. Light and dark, despair and euphoria, every paradox of human existence combine into one enormous diatribe on the leaves of lined paper, sometimes making complete sense and sometimes utter gibberish.

My voracious hunger strong arms me back to the here and now.

I survey the wrath of liberation's math: three empty ballpoint pens plus two filled notebooks and one dulled pencil equals an all-encompassing catharsis.

I hurry downstairs to the Vat House and scarf down a burger and fries like I haven't eaten in months. Back in my room, I plunge backward onto my bed then stare at the ceiling as blankly as I have done a million times, but I am a different person now.

The writer inside me has been set free.

I am reborn.

****

The lift's doors open the following morning and I rush over to Jame with my arms spread wide squealing with delight, "Guess what, Jame?"

His eyes brighten, and he receives me in his arms. "My goodness, you are simply bubbling over this morning."

I nuzzle my chin into his chest and reveal, "There's an amazing reason for my glee. I am a writer."

"Undeniably, love. I knew it all along."

We release each other and Jame backsteps. "Let me

check out Kelly the writer."

I blush through my bliss while he gives me the once over and nods.

"Yup, 100 percent certain. You are a writer, and what we are going to experience today will further enhance your transformation into a true wordsmith. Are you ready?"

I knit my fingers with his and reply with certainty, "I've been ready for this my whole life."

We arrive at the riverfront and Jame declares, "We are going for a jaunt on the Dart today."

"The Dart? Is it like a subway?"

"It's a rail system, but it doesn't go underground."

I draw to a halt and point to the ground. "That symbol there, the triskele. What can you tell me about it?"

Jame tugs me toward the buildings so we don't obstruct foot traffic. "Ah, the triple spiral, also known as the triskele or the triskelion, the same pendant on your necklace. The spirals date back to the Neolithic era when they were carved into the Newgrange tomb as separate helixes. Take a photo while the crowd is thin."

"Super idea." I sidestep to the symbol etched into the cement near a drain hole. Layers of dirt have transformed the triskele's formerly white spiral waves to black. I focus and snap my camera's shutter then walk back to Jame, who stands one legged in flamingo-like fashion against a wall constructed from brickwork with his arms crossed. "You look like you stepped out of a catalog in that pose." I chuckle and snap a picture of him. "I took three pictures of the triskele, but only one of you."

"Makes perfect sense you took three. When the three

individual spirals combine to create the triskele, the symbol represents a journey, both physically and spiritually," he explains. "We can interpret the motion of the arms in several ways, depending on culture, religion, and history. Wiccans attribute the three spirals to mother, maiden, and crone, while Christians might attach the trinity of father, son, and holy spirit to them."

He broadens his arms. "We're each traveling a unique road, and we assign personal meanings to the symbols and moments we encounter along our individual realms of existence. Such is the case with the triskelion. To me, the three spirals represent the three stages of awareness and experience: life, death, and rebirth, or past, present, and future."

"I should have kept my pendant."

"I beg your pardon?" He raises his eyebrow. "It's hanging from your necklace, is it not?"

"I found a different triskele trinket right before I left for college at the inlet near my writing spot. I thought it was something special, a lucky charm if you will, and I believed my life would move forward in a positive direction after I found it, but it didn't. Last December, a week or so before Shannon died, I was up at the inlet stewing over the darkness that overshadowed much of my life like a storm cloud."

"And?"

"I can freely admit now my poor choices caused most of the darkness. But the triskele I found brought me nothing. No light, no answers, just nothing for so many years, and in a moment of frustrated haste, I hurled it into the inlet. I guess I was hoping for a revival of sorts by relinquishing the cursed pendant to the ocean's waves."

I touch the triskele charm suspended by the silver

chain around my neck. "Less than two weeks after tossing mine into the inlet, Shannon's sister gave me this necklace, right after her funeral service ended. It was Shannon's, and Deirdre had no clue about the one I lobbed into the water. She said her gut instinct told her I needed this necklace." I squint toward the sky, my sunglasses concealing my misty eyes.

"The triskelion clearly chose you. It speaks to you and is using the universe to guide you."

"I believe you." I release an intentional exhale and cock my head toward him. "Okay, okay. Let's do this. Which way to the Dart?"

He clasps my hand and tugs me toward the right. "This way, to Tara Street Station."

We board a half-filled olive-green train car with large rectangular windows, and after we sit, he remarks, "We will be disembarking at the Dun Laoghaire station."

I study the route map posted on the wall. "Where is Done Leery? I see Dun Lag-oh-hair but no Leery."

He laughs. "Dun Laoghaire is how the name of the town is pronounced in Irish, or Gaelic. The town's name changed to Kingstown in the early 1800s but changed back to Dun Laoghaire in 1920."

"Oh," I flush and giggle. "How do you say the one spelled H-o-w-t-h?"

"Hote."

"Booterstown?"

"Same."

"Monkstown?"

"Same, but it's full of monks."

"Really?"

He snickers. "You're funny, Kelly."

The scenery outside the train car transforms from

city to seascape right before my eyes. I draw in my breath when I observe a length of sand with water a long way off and exclaim, "I wasn't aware Dublin had such beautiful waterscapes."

"Dublin's views along the strand are breathtaking, and the tides are truly something to behold. At high tide, the sea laps right against the retaining wall directly on the other side of the tracks, but at low tide, the water recedes as far out as half a mile or more. The Irish Sea's extreme and fast-moving tides have held many strand walkers prisoner."

I gesture toward the window and ask, "We just passed a round building made from tan cinder blocks. What can you tell me about it?"

"Those are Martello Towers. The Irish government built them along the coast during the nineteenth century to defend from potential invasions by Napoleon. There's a rather famous one we will visit later, one you might recognize from something."

"Whatever you are referring to must have slipped my mind. Tell me more."

He nods with a slight smirk. "You'll just have to wait and see."

It's got to have something to do with Joyce, but I don't want to ruin the air of mysterious anticipation, so I grin without saying anything.

The train slows and Jame announces, "This is our stop." He presses the flashing green button to open the door, then he leads me through the station and out to the streets of Dun Laoghaire. Bells from a nearby church announce the top of the hour by chiming loudly, and as we follow the road to the water, the sun shines warm and bright upon us.

My eyes grow, and I want to gallop. "Magnificent. With those piers, it's almost like…"

"Your inlet, love?"

"Yes." I pirouette in glee. "It's like you have given me a part of home, a part of who I am, the Dublin version of the Smuggler's in my soul."

The East and West piers resemble a crab's legs as each curves toward the other, with several sailboats moored inside the harbor found within. An orange-topped lighthouse towers at the end of the East Pier, its twin save for a green top diagonally across from it on the tip of the West Pier. The green, white, and orange Irish flag flies with honor above their respective lantern rooms.

"Can we walk all the way out to the lighthouse?"

"Of course."

If I could, I would capture the harbor with its aquamarine water and everything on the pier in a snow globe so I might magically return here whenever I wish.

While we make our way along the East Pier toward the lighthouse, Jame provides details about the landscape surrounding us. "Howth is across the way. Remember, it's spelled H-o-w-t-h, not H-o-t-e. Howth is a fishing village, and the white, miniscule lighthouse is the Bailey Lighthouse."

"The white lighthouse, there it is." I squint. "There to the left, the red blotch in the water. Is that another one?"

"Yes, the Poolbeg Lighthouse is the red building, and those two striped chimneys are the Poolbeg Stacks, or officially, the Poolbeg Generating Station. The stacks have been out of commission for years, but many citizens are against having them removed because they are such an iconic part of the Dublin landscape. In Joyce's time, that area was known as the Pigeon House. Stephen Dedalus' route took him past it in *Ulysses*. Recall the 'snotgreen sea'?"

My jaw dropped. "Is this really the 'snotgreen sea'?"

"Yes, indeed. And if you are excited by the sea, well, today is only going to get better," he hints with a mischievous smirk.

I nudge his side with my elbow. "Oh yeah? How much better?"

"It will be remarkable."

He nods toward an approaching blue fishing trawler. "See the boat, there? It is named the 'Jennie G.' My mate, Dylan, has worked on that boat since we were wee lads. He's now a third-generation sea captain."

"Similar fishing boats travel through Smuggler's Inlet at home. Many are local, but some are transients who need to unload their catch, escape the weather, or rest for the night."

"All kinds of vessels travel past here every day: ferries and cruise ships, tall ships, container ships, fishing vessels like the 'Jennie G,' you name it. Dublin and Howth are two very busy ports, and occasionally, larger sea crafts will moor right here in Dun Laoghaire, too."

When we come to the end of the pier, I run my hand over the cinder wall bathed with age surrounding the lighthouse's base. As a vitality ever so lightly emits from my fingers and travels through my arms and down my legs, it is like I am touching sandstone for the first time.

"You weren't kidding, Jame. My awareness is amplified, for sure."

"With your new appreciation for the magic of the

present moment, just imagine how much your life is going to improve."

I rotate my palms toward the sky and sigh. "So much wasted time."

"Let such thoughts go. If you don't, you will never be able to fully appreciate the present." He shakes his head. "The past made you who you are now, a lovely writer and a student of life with a new zest for existence, and led you here, to this pilgrimage of awakening. No regrets and no looking back."

One more lightning bolt of electricity leaves every hair on my body standing at attention. "This has already been a day like no other, and it's not even noon," I say before we trek back toward town.

"The blue-and-white truck there has deadly crepes. Let's stop for lunch."

"Deadly? You're not trying to kill me, are you?"

"You'll understand the Irish meaning of deadly when you take a bite."

And, boy, do I.

My palate overflows with satisfaction and I ascertain "deadly" is synonymous with "delectable" when I sink my teeth into my berry and cream crepe. I pan the pier while I devour the deliciousness. Several men and women donned in professional attire also enjoy their lunch al fresco alongside the water, while some read newspapers or engage in business deals on their phones. A couple engrossed in their novels ignore the mothers pushing their babies in strollers or the helmeted children who zip by on their scooters with their parents in tow.

When I finish eating, I scribble about my surroundings in my journal but pause when my mind hits a speedbump. "I wish I could find the words to accurately describe what I smell right now, the clean marine air and the sweet crepes and the intoxicating flowers combining to create an enchantingly aromatic showpiece."

"You just did, love."

"I guess you're right."

"You've just taken another step toward becoming the writer you're meant to be, which is long overdue. And speaking of long overdue…"

Jame takes a beat-up notebook from his rucksack and joins me in writing. A squawking gull lands at my feet to divert our attention and slow our pens after an hour or so passes. I stretch my legs to get my blood flowing again. "This is the first time I think I ever wrote in the company of someone else, other than random bystanders or sitting in a classroom."

"This is a first for me, too. I can't remember the last time I lost myself in my own writing."

I twist my back a few times, then I catch sight of something in the distance. I point and exclaim, "Look, there's one of those round towers like we passed on the train. What's it again, a marshmallow tower?"

"No, love. It's a Martello tower," Jame corrects me through his laughter. "That tower, in particular, is one of the more famous ones."

"Oh yeah?" I tilt my head. "What's so special about it?"

"Let us head there so you can find out."

We stroll the promenade alongside the sea and Jame nods to the right. "There, see it?"

Next to a sign for Link Road, I spot a bush shaped like a man with a cane. "Is that supposed to be James Joyce?"

"Precisely. The crude and misshapen replica might be the singular tree version of James Joyce in the world. Now, the sign with the arrow pointing in the same direction we are heading. Read it."

I step up to the black sign atop the metal post and squint as I read, "James Joyce Martello Tower." I pivot toward him and roar, "The James Joyce Martello Tower?"

"Without a doubt. If Shannon went to only one place here in Dublin, my money would be on that tower. *Ulysses* opens there, in the first chapter when Stephen Dedalus lived with Buck Mulligan, but more importantly, Joyce actually lived there too, albeit for only a week or so."

Jame clutches both of my shoulders with his hands and stares straight into my eyes so deeply I swear I can feel his presence in my soul. "It is important you continue alone. Allow Shannon's spirit to guide you along the route to the tower taken by Dedalus and Joyce."

"No, Jame," I object. "I want you to come with me."

A crisp gust smacks my face and I hear Shannon's voice full of cool sassiness in my ears. "Keep going."

"On second thought"—my body shakes—"maybe you are right. Maybe I do need to do this on my own."

He gestures with his arms and clarifies, "Stay straight on this walkway. When you reach the large, white rock up there, read its inscription then follow the road named Sandycove Point. It will bend left then slant up, and you'll pass The Forty Foot on your left, there's a sign for it. Continue upward and the tower will be on your right after the road curves again."

He leans his mouth toward mine and our lips

tenderly meet. The innocent kiss kindles an inferno firing from my toes through my crown. We separate and he says, "Take your time, love. I'll wait right here on this bench for you."

I am awestruck, my legs weak from both passion and anticipation, and I slightly stumble. Jame steadies me and we share a sincere giggle. "I'll be back," I murmur.

I breathe the sea air deep into my lungs, shut my eyes, and let the guiding zephyrs envelop me like a comforting shawl. The serene aqua water lightly laps the shoreline and I savor every step forward. When I arrive at the rock Jame mentioned, I read its inscription.

" '…he gazed southward over the bay, empty save for the smokeplume of the mailboat vague on the bright skyline, and a sail tacking by the Muglins.' This tree was planted by Councillor W.C. Willoughby An Cathaoirleach corporation of Dun Laoghaire on 18 May 1983 to mark the centenary of the birth of James Joyce."

The significance of this encounter astounds me.

Here I am, in Dublin, to honor Shannon's legacy and to look through her eyes. In turn, Shannon led me to this exact spot where her favorite author's words are forever engrained into the earth's soul along the Irish Sea. I pick up two stones near my feet and place them in my pocket before I continue my trek.

Several locals of all ages jump into the sea at Sandycove Beach even with the cool breeze, which would have driven people away from the beaches and bays back home. A gentleman who appears to be in his seventies tosses his cane to the side, slides his goggles over his eyes, and leaps into the water like an excited child.

What a lesson to behold. Let my surroundings invigorate me while living every possible moment.

I hike up the inclined Sandycove Point to a rusty sign with peeling paint proclaiming this The Forty Foot. The mandate imposed by a different generation granting swimming permission solely to gentlemen has clearly been annulled as several women alongside the men leap from the cliffs and frolic in the rough sea breakers battering the rocky wall.

The horizon supporting three colossal boats once again captivates my sight, and as I perceive a faint bellow, shivers shoot down my backbone. The echo from one of the ship's horns travels the distance over the splashing water and becomes a cherub's song of sorts in my ear. A smoke plume rises from the ship in the center and a sail to the south symmetrically balances the scene.

"…the smoke plume of the mailboat vague on the bright skyline…"

Joyce actually wrote this part of my story over eighty years ago, my incredulity euphoric and my revelation undoubtedly orchestrated by Shannon. I choke back tears and my gaze remains glued on the boats as part of me doesn't want this moment to end.

When my instincts dictate it's time to continue my expedition, I march upward along Sandycove Point's curve to the right and take each step with conviction. My heart's eagerness and my soul's inner wisdom both convey the Tower will be an ending and a beginning, and the destination I have been searching for my entire life.

And there it is.

The James Joyce Tower and Museum.

A sliver of sunlight breaks through the shroud of clouds and glistens on the enormous bastion like a beacon. A flash of memories rush through my mind and I allow them to have their final encore: the losses, the victories, the floundering, the worthlessness, the words, the abuse and degradation, every single experience leading me to the here and now.

It is time.

I step over the proverbial line from my old life and into my new. Shivers hot and cold race over my skin and my tummy floods with a thrilling rollercoaster-like exhilaration.

I scamper up the two gray steps made from granite-like paver stones then into the cylinder fortress, where I make chit chat with the volunteer manning the admission counter. She also hails from New Jersey and relocated to Dublin after retiring from her forty-year career as a private high school English educator.

Oh, Shannon, you so have your hand in this.

"You're in luck," she tells me. "We're not very busy today. The Tower is empty right now, so take advantage of the solitude."

I depart the counter and round the corner to enter what Shannon would consider to be the holy grail of James Joyce. I study Joyce's canes, suitcases, and other artifacts he owned on display behind glass cases and frames, including a simple, brown-stroked watercolor of Leopold Bloom painted by Roger Cummiskey in 2004 based on a sketch Joyce made of Bloom in 1923. There's a bookcase with well over a hundred different printing volumes of *Ulysses*, and I bet there's a copy in every language on those shelves.

I climb the narrow spiral staircase to the second floor and breeze into the exact room where Joyce himself lived and the same room where *Ulysses* opens. The room is laid out as it might have appeared during Joyce's short-lived tenure as a resident, with a hammock in the right corner, a simple bed along the back wall, and a center table adorned with bottles, food replicas, and blue and white porcelain tea cups. A ceramic black panther about three feet high stands on guard in the fireplace.

The panther.

I laugh as I think about the story Shannon told me about one of Joyce's roommates who woke in the middle of the night and fired a gun into the fireplace because he thought he saw a black panther there. The event terrified Joyce, who departed the tower for good almost immediately.

I deliberately inhale with hopes the same molecules that enveloped Joyce will permeate my soul, then I exhale and let my lips ride its vibration.

Only one place in the Tower remains for me to explore.

I ascend the last flight of tight cylindrical, concrete stairs and worm my way through a narrow gateway teeming with dust and dirt to the outside top level of the tower. The edifice boasts a running track for a cannon and a base in the center supporting a navy-blue flag with three gold crowns blowing wildly at the top of its pole.

I gently brush one of the smooth yet heavy brass rings hanging every few feet along the enclosure with my fingertips and think about Buck Mulligan's mock mass with his shaving dish at this exact spot. My thoughts turn inward, and after a few moments of uninterrupted reflection, I peer over the upper wall. With Dun Laoghaire to my left and the sea incredibly aqua, I trace the route I took, and Jame, sitting on his bench, is no bigger than a grain of rice from this vantage. My eye locates another lighthouse in the sea and the route to Dalkey on the right.

I appear to be utterly alone on the landing, but the wind gusts tell me otherwise.

The time has come for my testimonial, and I speak to the heavens.

"Shannon? Are you here? Can you hear me?"

A waft of air caresses my face with its invisible fingers and subtly replies, "Yes," into my ear.

"Shannon, my friend, my life began when yours ended. The times that almost killed me, that filled me with shame and self hatred, you showed me the reasons for enduring. I see through your lenses of love and fortitude and stand here triumphant.

"I'm no longer escaping from, or a spectator to, my life.

"I am running the race.

"And if I falter, I will rise again and clear those hurdles, a thousand times if needed."

Memories slip from my eyes, every one of their wet trails atingle from the wind, and I continue my tribute. "I live for you rather than mourn for you. You'll forever be my guide, my mentor, and my friend. The time has come for me to look through my own eyes and to be who I am. Right here, this moment is my ending and my beginning, my past, present, and future all rolled into one. This fucking amazing journey, my God, it stems from you and leads to me. Now I know why I came here. The light, the dark, midnight, the wave is here, and I'm not sleeping. I set your spirit free, my beautiful friend, with my eternal devotion and everlasting gratitude, as I embark upon my next chapter." I impulsively unclasp Shannon's triskele necklace from around my neck and heave it toward the sea.

A family of four shimmies through the confined rectangle portal onto the landing. I smear my tear-streaked face with my arm and depart the Tower's highest level just as a purple butterfly lands on the brass ring I stroked then glides into the wind.

Chapter Three

"Well, well, who is this exquisite bird running toward me?" Jame cheerfully asks as he rises from his bench. "She sure resembles Kelly, but there's something brilliantly different about her now."

I throw my arms around him. "Oh, Jame, I can't even begin to describe what I just experienced. I'm a new person, inside and out, and finally free to be who I really am."

"You are simply glowing."

"How did you know I needed to go alone?"

He slyly smiles. "The moment I first saw you in front of the museum, disheveled as you were, my instincts told me you were on some kind of personal quest. Then, after you shared your most intimate secrets with me, the loss of your husband and the details surrounding your pilgrimage here to honor your friend, well, let's just say our sculs need each other right now."

My heart sinks a little. "Just right now?"

"We don't want to ruin this moment by making things more complicated. Your life changed today, right?"

"Yes, it certainly did."

"For the better?"

"Definitely."

"Well, let's not poison a positive vibe with talk of the future or the past. Let's celebrate the present, the here and the now."

"Yes, we should celebrate. What do you have in mind?"

"How about a mouthwatering dinner at one of the best pubs on the planet? It's just a short walk away in Monkstown."

"Perfection."

We traipse the same route we took earlier along our backtrack to Monkstown and take advantage of low tide beside the Dun Laoghaire strand. The sea trinkets are very different from those I find along the beaches at home. I collect over a dozen tiny bright yellow spiral shells and twenty-seven sea glass pieces of varying blue hues. I clutch the last one tight in my hand and gaze upward with a memory of eyes the exact shade calming me.

"You okay, love?"

"Yes." I smile and drop the sea glass I gathered into my pocket. "Perhaps the best I've ever been."

Jame reclaims my hand into his, and we soon arrive at a restaurant named The Purty Kitchen. Over dinner, we learn we both like poetry by Simon Armitage and share a formidable distaste for that awful book, *Ethan Frome*. I groan with delight after the first taste of my succulent ten-ounce steak topped with melted Kerrygold. "This, right here is superb," I say with my mouth full as I bounce my fork on my plate. "Pairing it with Bewley's decadent strawberry shortcake would be the most perfect meal."

I cross my legs and end up knocking my knee on the underside of the thick, wooden table. I wince and while rubbing it, it dawns on me our server is the sole person taking or bringing orders in a room filled with patrons.

"Look—" I gesture toward her. "—she's got every table, but nobody is complaining about the slow service."

"Dubliners have a different approach to life. We go out for a meal for both sustenance and to spend time with others," he schools me. "Eating out is an event, whether it is breakfast, lunch, or dinner. We value the time we spend with our family, our friends, and sometimes, with just ourselves, so there's no rush. If we have to wait for our food or the cheque, it just means we have more time together."

"Life at home would be so much better if Americans adopted the same mindset instead of rush, rush, rushing all the time."

Jame settles our bill, and as we make our way outside, he says, "Why can't it be? The next time you're with friends or family, or even eating by yourself, consider this occasion here. Let the moment exist for what it is and treasure it as you would treasure your life."

"How did I get so lucky to cross paths with you?"

"The universe knows what it's doing." He encloses me in the crux of his arm and tugs me closer. "When we open ourselves up to it, it provides what it knows we need. Shannon played a hand in the universe's guidance of you, while I have no doubt Mam assisted with mine."

"Really? How so?"

"Mam idolized Joyce, same as Shannon. When you talk about her, I picture my mam in heaven with her, two peas in a James Joyce pod, and they are having a great deal of fun together."

He pauses, and when our eyes meet, my stomach flutters soar. I gently lean in as he does likewise, and I quake when our lips touch.

Tender.

Soft.

Then scorching.

His hands stroke my back, then pull me closer, and I melt in his scorching embrace.

We separate and the passion in his irises sends sparks down my spine.

We lock hands and amble to the Monkstown Dart Station under the first traces of the day's twilight without saying a word. An unspoken eagerness radiates from both of us on the train ride back to Tara Street Station, a passionate hunger with a side of frivolity pulsing through our bodies, and it takes every ounce of my willpower to hold myself back from jumping Jame's bones right then and there on the train.

We hurry hand in hand to Bloom's Hotel, through the lobby, and enter the lift to the third floor in silence. Before the door to my room closes fully, we melt into each other while stumbling to the bed. Our repressed animalistic instincts take over, and we rip off each other's clothes. We become one as I writhe in rhythm, and he dances inside me, and I climax with guttural moans composed of absolute euphoria.

The night is two weeks long if it is a day, every interlude of making love passionately different from the last. From tender and loving to wild and fiery, we experience the entire scale of sexual satisfaction from one end of the spectrum to the other. We exchange no words until sunrise when I roll over and become lost in his eyes.

"What do you see?" Jame murmurs.

"Your soul."

"What does it say to you?"

"We'll both remember this moment forever."

"For certain, love."

I drift asleep in his arms while the world outside begins its day.

****

I stir awake to Jame softly stroking my cheek. "What time is it?" I groan while I stretch.

"It's about one in the afternoon."

I kiss him then say, "You've got to be starving."

"Come to think of it, I could eat the twelve apostles. Should I run downstairs to fetch coffee and something to nosh?"

"Sounds great. I'll take a shower, but first…" I tug Jame toward me and our mouths canoodle before we emerge giggling from the covers.

He departs on his coffee-and-food mission while I shower, and after I dress, I gobble down my scone in four bites. He raises his eyebrow and quips, "Apparently I wasn't the only one who was famished."

"I was hungrier than I thought. I should probably charge this." I connect my phone's charging wire to the power converter I plugged into the wall. After I turn it on and it connects with my cell service provider, it vibrates like crazy with notifications. I furrow my brow and mutter, "What in criminy?"

"Everything okay?"

"It's a ton of missed calls from both my brother and my dad. I'm sorry, but I have to contact Christian," I say while dialing his number.

"Finally," my brother scolds when he answers. "Where have you been? Dad and I have been worried sick and were just about ready to file a missing person's report."

"Sorry, Christian. I turned my phone off."

"Obviously. I'm just glad you're safe. Listen, when are you planning to come home from Ireland?"

"I'm supposed to fly home tomorrow night. Why?"

"I don't mean to ruin your trip—" He exhales loudly. "—but Mom died yesterday."

The bed catches me as I fall. "What?"

"She suffered a massive stroke in her sleep. Even though neither of us was on good terms with her, I figured you'd want to know." Christian proceeds to provide the details for my mother's arrangements, which I scribble down on the back of the scone's bag.

Fuck.

Shit fuck damn fuck dammit all to hell.

I lower my head into my hands, the bliss of the past twenty-four hours promptly shattered.

"I'm so sorry for your loss, love." He sits next to me and takes my hand into his. "What are you going to do?"

I can't find my voice.

And I can't believe this is happening.

He rubs my back and I rasp through my sobs, "She's positively despicable, but I have to go. I don't suppose…"

"No"—he closes his eyes and gingerly shakes his head back and forth—"please don't suppose."

My bottom lip quivers. "But I don't want this to end."

"Neither do I, but life has dealt us its cards, love. I'm not a destination. I am merely a brief yet intense chapter of a future bestseller written in indelible ink."

The sun streams in through the window and creates a bar of gold sunshine shining directly in front of me. I latch onto Jame with a yearning to remain protected by his secure arms forever.

Enduring the Waves

****

I change the reservation for my flight home, and after I throw my belongings into my suitcase, Jame accompanies me to Dublin Airport. He offloads my luggage from the taxi outside Terminal One, and I exhale heavily. "This wasn't how I hoped this adventure would end."

"Me either." Jame holds me tight in his arms. "I never would have guessed our lives would have connected like this. While our futures will diverge, you will eternally own a part of my heart."

"Mine, too. Thank you for helping me remember how to smile and for helping me find myself."

"It wasn't me. It was you. You found yourself, guided by Shannon."

"No," I whimper. "It was you, too. She led me to you, and you led me to myself." I breathe in his scent as deep as I can before I ask, "Will I ever see you again?"

Jame doesn't answer me. Instead, he cups my chin and locks me in an osculation for the ages.

I don't want to let him go.

As we separate, he quavers and his voice cracks. "Take care of yourself. Never forget Dublin's lessons. And always be proud of who you are, love." He gives me one last kiss on my forehead, shields his face with his hands after shutting the door, and disappears as the taxi drives away.

With weepy, bloodshot eyes and a crestfallen spirit, I head to the ticketing counter for American-bound flights with my luggage in one hand and my boarding pass in the other.

Ten hours later, I am home in Waterville but too keyed up to sleep, so I unpack my suitcase. Visions from my mission abroad flash through my memory, gossamer and dreamlike, so much so I question whether everything really happened or if it was all a grand illusion.

When I throw my jeans onto the laundry pile, a little white bag tumbles out of them with a note and a velvet drawstring sack inside. My eyes water as I recognize Jame's handwriting.

Love, I do not have much time to write this. I have no doubt the person you are right now, as you are reading this, is a writer. Life is real and never has the fairy tale ending, but we are the wiser because it doesn't. Take what you have learned about yourself and about life and let it be your greatest inspiration. I know I am a better person right now because I met you, and I hope you feel the same. Our souls will always share a connection, even though this chapter has ended. Remember Dublin as you continue moving forward. Let your past and your present inspire your future as a writer. That light, it will always be shining ahead for you.

Inside the sack is an engraved pewter triskelion bracelet with an inscription on its inside, "Let the mysteries of the universe guide you. Forever light, J."

Cue the teardrops.

When did Jame buy it, or have it engraved, or even write the note? I was with him almost every second of my last forty-eight hours in Dublin.

My wet eyes find the three notebooks I purchased at Easons scattered on the couch where I dumped my carry-on. I stretch for the empty mint green one and frantically write through my sorrow for hours.

****

Christian, Dad, and I arrive at Bolton's Funeral

Home the following afternoon at the same time, and we gather in the parking lot. "Hey, sis." Christian hugs me. "Sorry you had to cut your Dublin spree short."

I wince inside at hearing Dublin. "It's not your fault. Is Diego here?"

"No, he's got an important meeting tomorrow, but he said to tell you he's already throwing down the challenge of hooking a bigger fish than you the next time you visit."

"Sorry about this, kiddo," Dad unnecessarily apologizes. "The one time you actually go and do something for yourself, and life has to chuck a wrench at you."

"No worries. I'm kind of surprised you came, but then again, I'm surprised any of us are here."

"I spent more than half of my life with Diana. The right thing to do is to pay my respects."

I tremble as visions from the last two times life forced me to visit Bolton's flit through my memory.

This time, though, is different.

This time, my soul's newfound independence and wisdom keep me in check. I walk into the funeral home exuding confidence with my brother on my left and Dad on my right.

Hysterical screams resound from the viewing room. "Oh, Diana, why did you have to leave me?" Charlene unexpectedly whips her head in our direction and shrieks, "Why the hell are you people here?"

I clench my jaw while Dad raises his hands and implores, "Charlene, please. No drama. Let us pay our respects in peace."

"You all hated her," she roars from the room into the lobby and continues her tirade, "I was the only one who truly loved her."

Jacques Bolton the funeral director emerges from his office.

"Charlene, we discussed this. They have a right to be here, same as you."

"Screw you, Jacques," she shouts then storms out of the building.

"All righty then." Christian's offhand comment breaks the tension.

"The public viewing will start in half an hour. Let me go in first to say my goodbyes in private," Dad says before lumbering into the viewing room.

Christian and I sit on a cream-colored sofa banked by small tables on each end. "So, how was your trip?" Christian wonders.

A twinge shoots through my body and a knowing smile creeps up from the corners of my mouth as I answer, "Absolutely amazing."

"I see. You're different, but in a good way."

"I am. It's going to take some figuring out, but I finally know the path I am supposed to follow."

"It's about time," he loudly proclaims, which prompts a loud shushing from Jacques Bolton the funeral director.

"I hated leaving Dublin, but I sure am glad to see you."

"Me too, sis."

Dad and Christian swap spots, with Dad sitting next to me while Christian pays his respects. I take Dad's hand into mine and whisper, "I'm blessed to be your daughter, Dad, and I'd like to let you in on a little secret. I'm a writer."

"I know." He kisses my forehead. "I've always

known."

Christian is teary when he emerges. His gesture signals it's my turn in the rotation.

Here goes nothing.

One step after another into the empty, cool room leads me to the front, where my mother's casket sits alone. Her hair is impeccable and her makeup flawless, as usual. I cringe because nothing was ever real about her, not even in death. Everything about my mother was fake, except for the dress she is wearing which is the same shade of nauseating pink as my horrendous prom gown.

I'm surprised, though, to find her face relaxed and without her trademark scowl or her saccharine smile, like the one she wore in the photograph taken of me a few days after the 1980s dropped anchor when I was just a baby.

I pry through my wallet, digging behind its various plastic card inhabitants, and feel the creased corner of the image. Just like that blue bottle, my soul is the sole entity who knows this photograph took up residence in my wallet when I was eight years old. As I slide the picture into the room's light for the first time in years, my whole being inside and out quivers.

Within its impeccably faded corners, there I am, all tiny and bundled up in my mother's arms at Smuggler's with a dusting of snow on the ground. The image captured a speck of a moment in time, one the casual onlooker might mistake for a tender moment between mother and child.

But such a sublime occasion never existed, no matter how much I wanted to believe it did.

Behind her lies and counterfeit countenance,

manipulation and narcissism converted her shame into tyranny.

The corners of my eyes become moist when I realize I will never learn the identity of my biological father. My mind screams for answers, and I grumble, "Thanks for nothing."

I dab my eyes with a tissue, then resume my farewell. "I take that back. Thanks for giving me life, and for the pain and the scars. My life sentence of humiliation at your hands has now been pardoned, and you can never hurt me again."

I place the worn photograph next to her in the casket, lightly stroke her cheek with my fingertips, then turn my back on her forevermore.

We remain at the funeral home for the duration of the viewing, much to Charlene's chagrin. I'd say about a dozen mourners come to pay their respects, and I don't recognize any of them. As per my mother's request, this is the sole opportunity for in-person condolences. She will be cremated, and Charlene will take possession of her ashes.

Kind of a sad showing, but she deserves it.

Dad, Christian, and I have dinner at The Hurricane after the viewing and relish every moment we are together as a family, considering the circumstances. At one point, Christian criticizes the service is too slow. I think about The Purty Kitchen and explain the wait is a blessing because we have more time to enjoy each other's company. "You always had the wisdom in the family, sis," he said.

Christian and I plan to meet at Smuggler's at ten tomorrow morning and spend the day together. Dad declines our invitation to join us for tomorrow's shenanigans because he has to work. "Besides," he says, "I think you two could use some brother-sister time."

I struggle into the townhouse at almost eleven, exhausted and spent from both the stress and the jetlag. I throw on a comfy t-shirt and sweat shorts, and when I brush my hair, the woman returning my gaze in the mirror is strong and at peace in this moment, and I am damn proud of her.

I curl up with my notebook but fall fast asleep before I can scribble a single word.

****

There is something I must do in order to properly christen this new season of my life.

The late-June morning is already brassy gray and uncomfortably balmy by sunup, with humidity hanging thick in the air. The colorless atmosphere mirrors my revelation that, at times, sadness and melancholy must coexist with positivity and purpose.

My car's tires grind on the sand-and-pebble driveway slithering through the monochrome Saint Michael's Cemetery, and I pull over near a line of white rose bushes. With the weight of the universe upon me, I depart my vehicle into the heavy clamminess and advance upon Shannon's grave with one of the stones I pilfered from the footing of the Muglins rock alongside the sea in Sandycove bouncing in my pocket.

However, I hesitate because an old woman dressed in black from head to toe is standing right in front of Shannon's headstone.

Damn. I expected to be alone.

A paradox of emotions swirls within me, selfishness because I feel violated, and guilt because I do not want to interrupt the mystery woman's visit. I'm torn between trudging forward or retreating and coming back another time when a thick Irish accent shatters the copious silence, "Come here, my child."

I sharply inhale and she motions me forward with her left index finger while still staring straight ahead. "Yes, you. Join me, please."

I do as she instructs and scurry to stand next to her. I'm certain she must hear my heart because it feels like it's going to pound right out of my chest.

"Such a shame," she says after a momentary reticence while shaking her head from side to side. "Such wasted talent."

"What do you mean?"

"You and her." She points to Shannon's headstone, then she cocks her head toward me and points in a like manner to me. Our eyes connect, and her familiar shamrock greens enthrall me so, I am spellbound.

"Once you write chapter one, everything will fall into place," she proclaims with certitude.

Every single one of my hairs stands on end, and I almost gag on my words, "What…what did you…just say?"

She takes my hands into hers and repeats, "Once you write chapter one, everything will fall into place, dear."

The energy from her soft, supple hands clasping mine sparks a sense of Deja vu that permeates every cell in my being while her words render me motionless.

The elder releases her grip and fumbles with her dress pocket. Her wrinkled fingers place something in the palm of my right hand, gently fold my fingers over it, and squeeze mine with an incredible warmth spreading up my arms and into my center.

I am rendered motionless.

She turns her head to me, and with an auspicious twinkle in her eyes, she releases her grip and turns around. Her feet shuffle on the gravel walkway behind me, the crunch of her light tread growing fainter with each of her steps.

After both my breath and my pulse revert to normal and I can move again, I pivot and call into the void, "Hello? Are you here?"

The old woman has vanished.

I peel back each finger to discover Shannon's triskele necklace resting in my palm, the one I hurled from the top of the James Joyce Tower, and I have to steady myself.

But...how?

A gust of wind almost identical to the one alongside the Irish Sea swats my face and encompasses me like a twister before fading just as swiftly as the woman. I fasten the delicate chain around my neck and close my eyelids while stroking the triskele in awe.

A singing mockingbird circles me back to the present moment. I set the stone from my pocket on top of Shannon's headstone and whisper, "Hey, you. From deep within the essence of my being, thank you. I love you, my friend."

As I go to leave, my eye catches something fluttering in the air. A lively little lavender butterfly lands on the stone I just placed, adjusts its wings, then floats away to become the lone speck of color shimmering against the breezy gray clouds.

****

With my brother's year-round Key West tan and natural sun-bleached hair, I have no problem spotting him drawing in his sketchbook when I park along

Smuggler's Inlet. I sneak up behind him and garble in a low tone while sticking my finger into his back, "Listen, mister, don't move or you're dead."

"I'm terrified," he flatly answers without breaking his concentration, unfazed by my idle threat. We then both crack up, and he pats the open bench to his right. "Take a seat, sis."

I park myself beside him and observe the incoming current is full of spearing. "Check it out, Christian. Remember when you would use your seining net to catch spearing for Old Man Massey's bait shop?"

"I'd earn a nickel for every ten fish. Two hundred fish for a buck. Then that son of a bitch would sell them for a buck a dozen. Boy, was I a chump, or what?"

"You were just a kid."

"I know, but Massey really took advantage of me. Let me finish my sketch. I'll be done in a few."

"Sure thing."

As he adds detail to the already impressive fishing trawler on his sketchpad, I list every word I can to describe it on a page in my notebook. He tilts the finished drawing toward me, and I'm mystified. "I forgot how talented of an artist you are."

"Who would have thought doodling in every middle and high school class would lead to a career? Last week, I found out the Greater Key West Area Art Society selected me to paint the mural for their new headquarters after they saw my work at the visitor center." He tears the trawler drawing out of his sketchbook and hands it to me. "Here, I want you to have this."

"I'm going to frame it." I place his drawing inside of my notebook.

"Come on," Christian scoffs. "It's average at best."

"It is wonderful, and it will be a permanent reminder of this exact moment with my not-so-little brother."

"You're crazy, sis, but I love you anyway." He grinds his knuckle into my forehead like I used to do to him when we were kids. A party boat passes by with its rails full of anglers eager to catch fluke and whatever other legal bounty the sea would provide, and my gaze centers on the vessel's wake in the water.

"You okay?" he asks.

"Yes, just contemplating something you said."

"What did I say?"

"About making a living off your doodles. It is possible, then, to make ends meet from pursuing your passion?"

"It's been tough at times, but, yes, it can be done. Why should I waste my life doing something I'm not that into just for a paycheck? I might not be rich, but I'm happiest when I'm creating, and my time is valuable to me. I'm making a living by pursuing my passion of art and living a full life. I'm lucky to share it with someone who respects my talent and supports my endeavors. It's not just my job, it's who I am."

"I'm so proud of you."

"Sis, you're getting sappy. What's up?"

"Christian." I take a deep breath. "I am a writer. I know that now as well as I know my own name. Writing is and always has been the fire in my heart and in my soul, and I'm not afraid to be who I am anymore."

"Well, damn, Kelly," he chortles. "I've known that for, like, forever."

"And going to Dublin, the trip made me keenly aware I want to see and experience more than just what's here at the Jersey Shore. I don't want to be a lifelong hostage of my zip code."

"As you shouldn't."

"Then you understand when I admit I'm considering quitting my job as a teacher so I can travel and write full time?"

"Absolutely. From what you've told me, you are financially okay, right? Unless you squandered your inheritance and savings abroad?"

"I most certainly did not," I respond through a defiant sneer. "I've been very responsible with my finances and I'm not a spender. I'll be able to get by for a while without having to worry about money."

"Just kidding, sis. I commend you for your financial responsibility. Let me ask you one question. When do you feel most alive?"

Without even thinking, I blurt out, "When I'm writing."

"There's your answer. Write. Sit at Smuggler's and write. Wander the world and write. If it doesn't work out, you can always return to the classroom, but if your gut instinct is telling you to write, then write. This is your only life, right here, right now, so what makes you, you, sis."

I swiftly grab Christian with both of my arms, and after squirming at first, he returns my hug and says, "I'm craving Dom's Fries. You game?"

"Of course. No visit to Oldentown Beach is complete without indulging a container or five of Dom's Famous Fries."

We head to my old stomping grounds, but Dom is off for the day. Three hours pass in the blink of an eye because we talk so much. Once we settle our bill, Christian says, "I guess I should vamoose. Dad's giving me a lift to the airport tonight. Want to tag along for the ride?"

"I'd love to."

Dropping him off at the airport is an easy gig because he travels light. I say my goodbyes to my brother, and while Dad says his, memories from another airport farewell flash through my mind. I spot a billboard advertising a sale on flights to Dublin, and my heart simultaneously smiles and shudders.

****

The first thing I write after I get home from the airport is my resignation letter, which I deliver in person to my principal the following morning. He is disappointed about losing me but praises my conviction to follow my passion. I adhere to contractual procedure and give the district more than sixty days to find a replacement, so I am able to sever all ties with my former profession. As the Waterville High School building grows smaller in my rearview mirror, my phase as an educator concludes.

The heat and oppressive humidity negates writing at Smuggler's, so I head straight home to the townhouse.

But is it really my home?

When I open the door, the picture of Wayne standing with a beer on my first day of teaching develops in my mind as clearly as he stood almost two years ago. I gaze at the couch and there he is, nodding off with empty beer bottles haphazardly strewn below him on the carpet. I can hear the sizzle of the pork roll he's frying on the stove and my mouth waters from its hearty, one-of-a-kind aroma.

He is everywhere, and this is, in fact, his townhouse.

I warily tread down the hall and hover in front of the

door to the Smuggler's room, a door I have not opened since...

It boggles my mind how much my life has changed since Thanksgiving, and how much of a different person I am today than the woman who last closed that door.

I twist the cold glass knob with my hand, then slowly nudge the door ajar after the latch clicks open. I flick the switch on the wall and the stale, incandescent bulbs inside the recessed ceiling lights fracture the darkness. Cobwebs have connected the remnants of my destroyed laptop on the floor, covered the hole I punched into the mural, and laced across the window blinds' slats. The layer of dust coating everything becomes alive as I circle the room and scan the mural spanning all four walls.

This version of Smuggler's Inlet was never real.

It was pretend.

And it belonged to Wayne, just like everything else in the room.

Come to think about it, this version of my life was never real, either.

It was just as pretend, and like the tiny light bulbs that should be twinkling in the ceiling and at the end of the painted jetties, it has burned out.

And so, it is.

A remarkable intensity saturates my body out of the blue, and along with it, an indefinable yearning to move forward. Whereas minutes ago I stood frozen in front of the door, my body now springs into action. I struggle to lift the desk chair and drag its unwieldy carcass through the mugginess to the curb. I march back inside and dump the contents from one of the desk drawers into a large, black garbage bag without rummaging through it, then haul the drawer outside and drop it next to the desk chair. I continue emptying the room until all its former contents are waiting at the street for either someone else to give them a home or to be heaved into the municipal garbage truck.

I am a sweaty, panting, red-faced mess, but I'm not finished.

I stare down the mural with ire building inside me.

How the hell could I have allowed a place so dear to me to be replaced by a painted replica?

I storm to the utility closet and grab a paint can, a screwdriver, and a paint roller, then drop everything in the vacated room. The can's lid proves difficult to remove, and I fail to free it by jimmying it with the screwdriver. In a flash, I retrieve a hammer and bang it against the end of the screwdriver as hard as I can. The lid pops off and lands on the carpet paint side down, but I don't give a damn about ruining the formerly pristine rug with its beautifully woven ocean waves.

I force the roller into the can, raise it dripping and wet, and slide it across the inlet's seawall. In one fell swoop, I erase the fishermen and the seabirds and the little boy with the red bucket of fish. I dip the magic wand of a roller again, and this time, I make the surfers disappear. Another swipe eliminates the fishing boats on the horizon, along with Glenharbor's rocks.

In a jiffy, all four walls contain nothing more than a mass of thick and sloppy eggshell-white lines spattered in every direction with a few lingering paper-thin streaks of color peeking from behind them.

The mural's lifespan has concluded, and my time as a resident of this address with it.

My stomach transmits its hunger signal, so I grab

cold cuts, cheese, and mayo from the fridge, and slap two pieces of bread on a china plate I take from the cupboard.

The china.

This gaudy set of hideously flowered plates, and bowls, and saucers, and mugs from someone connected to Moira who I can't even remember.

That's it for them.

I set my sandwich fixings aside and head to the closet in the laundry room. When I yank open the door, the damn starfish Santa stored on the middle shelf sneers at me from its hook atop the metal shelves. I rip each of its arms off and dump its body parts into an empty box, which I carry back to the kitchen. I proceed to drop each piece of fine china into the box on top of the dismembered Santa. Some of the pieces shatter on impact, and those that don't, I blast with a hammer. I drag the box to the curb to join the relics from my former life.

Satisfied, I make my sandwich and eat off a paper plate while perusing the yellow pages and online directories for both a realtor and a handyman. I've done all I can with transforming the Smuggler's Escape back to a regular room, but I will need professional help stitching its scars by properly painting the walls, restoring the floors, and removing the malfunctioning tiny lights that have gone black.

On the way home from the airport last night, Dad mentioned he found an affordable and spacious condominium on the market over in Glenharbor. He plans on selling the house on Seacrest Court. Shannon always told me I didn't have to be stuck in Waterville forever, and she's right. My short-lived quest to Dublin awakened a fervent eagerness to visit new places and experience new cultures. Dad offered me a bedroom in his new condo, complete with a small alcove perfect for writing, so I can have a home port of sorts while traveling.

I will accept his offer.

Residing on the other side of Smuggler's, though, will take some getting used to.

Part of me wants to hop on a plane right now and go somewhere new, but with packing, and selling the townhouse, and getting settled with Dad, and writing…

Breathe.

Just breathe, and have faith.

It will come in time.

****

By the time October arrives, new owners reside in both the townhouse and the house on Seacrest Court, and Dad and I are settled in his Glenharbor condominium. Surfers of all ages cruise the swells spurred by a typical Jersey mid-autumn nor'easter on their boards, and they universally kindle an ache inside me to learn how to surf. I'm not much of a swimmer, so I enroll in an adult swim program at a local gym to strengthen my arms and legs. I also book a trip for early spring to a women's surf retreat in Costa Rica where beginners are welcome.

No more gaping at a mural for me. I want to be alive in the real thing and ride the waves as the salt water frolics over my skin.

The nor'easter blows out of town the same day I finish polishing my first novel's manuscript. I submit shorter pieces of creative nonfiction and personal essays to journals and magazines while querying agents and publishing houses with my novel.

My work is accepted here and there, but every

response to my novel is a rejection.

I don't let that stop me.

The rejections motivate me because they are evidence someone is actually reading my work but concurrently dishearten me because I am a human. Each one pushes me to revise my manuscript then send it back out into the trenches hoping for a bite.

After I receive rejection number fifty, I throw myself on my bed and wish for a crystal ball or a genie to tell me what to do. I muse about Jame and where he might be at this exact moment, then I scold myself for going down that rabbit hole. The roll of undeveloped film from Dublin tucked away in my closet teases me, and I wonder if I'll ever have the gumption to drop it off at the photo center or if I should just wing it into the garbage can or the inlet.

I bash my pillow with my fist a few times, then quench my desire for fresh air by taking a brisk walk down to Smuggler's with the ocean to my left. The afternoon is exquisite with just a few clouds dotting the sky. I carefully step over the goldenrod remnants swaying through the boulders and follow my well-tread path to the rock opposite my former writing spot. I close my eyes and allow the serenity of my surroundings and the salt air to cleanse my soul.

I am almost in a meditative state. My cell phone suddenly vibrates from inside my back pocket almost at the same time as an approaching bunker boat blares its horn at a rogue kayaker who has paddled into its course.

So much for trying to find peace.

With my Zen ruined, I grab my phone and find a voicemail notification flashing on its display. I do not recognize the New York City phone number and assume it's a telemarketer hocking some sort of warranty plan. While listening to the message, two seagulls loudly disputing ownership of a cracker tossed by a nearby child distract me but I swear I hear the words "agent," "manuscript," and "representing."

I press my left ear shut with my finger and listen to the message again.

"Good afternoon, Kelly. My name is Amanda Carolan. After reading the letter and manuscript you emailed to me, I would like to talk with you more about the possibility of representing you. Please return my call at your earliest convenience. Have a pleasant day."

I replay the message three more times to confirm I am not dreaming.

Another boat entering the inlet's mouth blasts its horn as I scuttle over the rocks and sprint home as fast as I can run.

I burst into the condo from nowhere and Dad yells, "Kelly, what's going on, for crying out loud?"

"Sorry I…startled you…everything's fine," I sputter out between my panting. "An agent…left me a message…she's interested in me."

"Wait, there's a problem with the sale of your townhouse? I thought it closed already?"

"It's a literary agent, Dad, not a real estate agent. I need to call her back."

"Oh, I understand. I'll go sit on the balcony so you can have some privacy."

After I make the call, I join him on the landing. He shifts his gaze toward me and says, "You look happy, so good news, I hope?"

"Well"—my grin grows—"I've got an appointment with a literary agent in New York City. Everything just feels right about this."

"Congratulations, kiddo." Dad walks down to the rosebush hedges with his shears in his hand, snips the last of the season's two roses, and hands them to me as he reenters the balcony. "Can I take you to The Hurricane to celebrate?"

"Absolutely."

****

While sitting at a table in New York City's Bryant Park, I check the time on my phone. I caught an extra-early train into the city to avoid being late, but I still have two hours to kill before my meeting with Amanda Carolan. Her office is in the building next to the New York Public Library. I'm wearing a brand new blue dress the color of water and carrying a classy yet professional black leather tote Christian sent me for good luck.

I'm not even the slightest bit nervous. It's like Dublin all over again—I know I am where I am supposed to be without any doubts or misgivings.

It's a gem of a morning, considerably warmer than it should be for the week before Thanksgiving, and I lose myself in writing about the Bryant Park scenes in my journal.

Out of nowhere, a shadow blocks the sunlight from shining on my page and I hear a masculine voice above me, "Excuse me, I don't mean to bother you, but my phone just fell into your purse."

I shift my head and gaze up into soothingly gentle eyes, brown with flecks of gold near the pupils, behind a pair of glasses. The tall, male owner of the eyes sports a husky build, dark brown hair, and an aura of kindheartedness. I flush and rescue his phone from my tote. "Here you go."

"If I reached into your purse, you would have surely thought I was a miscreant."

"Miscreant," I giggle. "Now, there's a good word."

After a short silence, the man remarks, "Your necklace. If you don't mind my asking, where did you get it?"

My fingertips caress the ridged spirals of Shannon's triskele. "It's a long story."

"My name is Sylas Jamison, and my grandmother, I swear she had the same necklace. I've got a meeting with clients in an hour, and hearing the story behind your necklace would be a wonderful way to pass the time."

I slide the empty bistro chair at my table toward him with my foot, its metal legs scraping against the concrete, and flash him a smile. "It's nice to meet you, Sylas. My name is Kelly Lynch, and I'm a writer."

Epilogue

"Think you're escaping and run into yourself. Longest way round is the shortest way home." James Joyce, *Ulysses*

Man, this has been quite a ride. From the edges of debilitating despair to this moment, to the here and now, I am still standing. I never surrendered to the turbulent darkness hovering over me like a storm cloud.

While the dark still shows up now and then, the light is actually visible in every moment. I just might have to readjust my focus or alter my vantage to perceive it, and it's much easier to see things differently when I'm not running away from life's trials but enduring them.

I consider everything I've seen and experienced while honoring Shannon by looking through her eyes. It didn't register at the time, but she died on December 29, the same day Joyce's masterpiece *Portrait* was first published.

That's not a coincidence.

At last, I am at peace with both my past and who I truly am—a writer.

I never expected James Joyce to have such a significant influence on my life. I'm not a superfan or anything of the sorts, but after Shannon opened my eyes, Joyce reinforced my awakening about the value of the present moment and the grandeur of everything I observe with my eyes, experience with my senses, and enlighten in my soul.

And I respect the hell out of him.

I'm still reconciling with loss, and some days are better than others. Instead of grieving for both Wayne and Shannon, I endeavor to allow their light to shine into mine. Wayne will always be my first love, and he emancipated me from my deplorable home life. On the other hand, Shannon helped me liberate myself from both my blindness and my self-deprecating prison cell.

Strangely enough, my friendship with her today is greater than ever and transcends the heavens of the afterlife. And believe me, she lets her feisty presence from within her parallel universe be known, perhaps through a random Joyce reference, or an unexpected triskele placed within my day, or a package of Kerrygold butter tumbling from the supermarket shelf in front of me for no reason whatsoever.

Shannon is still here, and I love it.

It's been a year since my first meeting with Amanda, and she's the perfect agent for me, forthright and bold, and excited to take a chance on an unknown writer. What are the odds she has a framed triskele with a Joyce quote underneath it hanging in her office, or she learned to surf as a kid at Glenharbor's surfing beach next to Smuggler's Inlet? The universe still spins its arms to guide me, that's for sure.

We are preparing for the release of my first novel next month with a press tour and a launch party already booked at The Hurricane, courtesy of Dad, Christian and Diego, who are both flying up for the celebration. My next project with Amanda will bring the antics of Kay and Ess to bookshelves with the eventual publication of the Benevolenters series.

Shannon's prophecy was correct.

Once I wrote chapter one by choosing to live, everything fell into place.

I keep in touch with both Del and Monica, and while I don't regret a minute I spent in the classroom, I don't miss it. My classroom wasn't a destination. It was merely a necessary detour, just like Jame.

The one who got away.

I wouldn't be human if I didn't get pissed off every now and then about not knowing the identity of my biological father. Sometimes, when I pass a man about Dad's age and our blue eyes meet, I wonder if he could be my biological father. The writer in me will become almost delirious and spin story after story in my mind about the man, but then my common sense levels out my fantasies.

He's out there, somewhere, and maybe the universe will someday unite us.

But maybe not.

I'm euphoric with hope about my still-developing story with Sylas and hooked on our narrative. We traveled together to Hawaii and also to Costa Rica on my second jaunt to that surf camp, a place which transformed my life just as much as Dublin did. I may be a terrible surfer, but when I am surfing, I am one with the water and ride the waves as best as I can.

When Sylas showed me his first grade school portrait taken when he was seven years old, my jaw dropped because he resembled the exact mental picture I drew of Kay's sidekick, Ess, in my Benevolenters stories. And he wasn't lying about his grandmother's necklace, either. She is wearing it in a picture of her taken in Dublin near the turn of the century and it is exactly like Shannon's. Grandma Jamison also bears a strikingly uncanny resemblance to that old woman I encountered at Shannon's grave.

Come to think of it, to the woman on O'Connell Street, too.

I'll be damned.

Life continually imitates art when I least expect it.

I shut my eyes and see, both inwardly and outwardly as Joyce advised, and I am living the hell out of this one, precious life I've been given. I've learned to honor both the dark and the light because their meshing and melding are the mainstay of my existence, and quite honestly, of human existence.

My journey may not have been all puppy dogs and rainbows, but it's all mine, and it's not finished yet.

In less than two months, I will celebrate my thirtieth birthday.

But this time, as I embark upon another voyage around the sun, I will do so knowing I matter to the universe. Within every moment exists the potential for a new and exciting episode to begin. Every sunrise will be an awakening, every wave a lesson, and every sunset a victory.

My journey is my purpose, and I will never stop riding its waves.

A word about the author...

Jill Ocone has been a high school communications/journalism and English teacher since 2001 and a writer/editor for Jersey Shore Magazine/Jersey Shore Publications since 2014. She loves making memories with her nieces and nephews, seeing new places, laughing with her family and friends, and sharing her Jersey Shore home with her husband. Enduring the Waves is her debut novel.

Thank you for purchasing
this publication of The Wild Rose Press, Inc.

For questions or more information
contact us at
info@thewildrosepress.com.

The Wild Rose Press, Inc.
www.thewildrosepress.com